Anna's Hunger Games

By Boyd Brent

Author contact:
boyd.brent1@gmail.com

Copyright: Boyd Brent

Preface

Welcome to Anna's Hunger Games. These games can start with a few thoughtless words. For me it took just five, planted like poisonous seeds within my mind: 'You're too fat to model.' That ridiculous comment brought a murderer into my life. Her name was Anna Rexia. Anna preys on the young mostly. Those with everything to lose. I wanted to live. And this is the story of what happened when I went in search of the knowledge I needed to destroy *her*.

Chapter 1

Okay. You're still listening, which means you have an inquiring mind. And maybe you've battled your fair share of inner demons, too. By inner demons, I mean *any* voice that has lived inside your mind and made you miserable by reminding you of something you wanted to forget. I hate to pull rank but the voice of my inner demon, Anna, was louder than most. Which explains why I had the following perspective about her: while Anna was a part of me, she was also *separate* from me. As you're about to discover, this became clear the moment I tried to defy her. By the end of our journey together, you're going to understand more about the nature of our inner demons (the things that truly make us unhappy) than you ever imagined possible. Sharing this knowledge has been my sole motivation for telling my story. And this is one instance where knowledge *is* power ...

My name is Hally Winters. I'm 17. And believe it or not, I've always been the sensible, easy going one in my family. So how could five words (spoken by a ditsy friend) have birthed a class A psycho inside my mind? Looking back, it had a lot to do with my being emotionally and physically spent. For starters, a flu virus had confined me to my bed for a week. I'd had *way* too much time to think. And I convinced myself that my boyfriend, the guy who meant everything to me, had been seeing someone else. On top of that, the family dog died. My kid sister, Sarah, cried herself to sleep in the next room all week. I guess it was a combination of all of the above that left me feeling so vulnerable. So it was that Anna loomed from the shadows, took me by my hand, and led me towards her hunger games, "*I know a way to make all the hurt go away,*" she whispered.

Anna grew quickly. It's ironic but she had the biggest appetite ever. She was ravenous in pursuit of her influence over me. The more we talked about stuff, and the more I listened, the louder she grew. Thanks to Anna, the impossible happened – I'd barely thought about my cheating boyfriend, Edward. So what if he'd been seen out with Charlotte again? Anna stamped on these worries with her size 17 jackboots. She said, *"Edward doesn't matter. He's beyond your control. And like I keep telling you, nothing beyond your control can make you happy."* Fears of botching my exams, disappointing my parents, letting down my friends: all quietened by Anna's whispers. Anna Rexia is a master manipulator. And she'd done a bang up job of convincing me that *she* was my voice of reason. *"People have told you that you could model? They're crazy. Simple as. Sophie was so right. You're way too fat now."* And then, one morning, she whispered, *"Crash diet."* She might just as well have told me to abandon ship. The ship in question was my 'normal' relationship with food. Stupid girl, I grabbed the faulty life jacket Anna handed me ... and threw myself over the side ... SPLASH! ... Gelug gelug like a mug.

Until Anna, I'd thought of myself as being too skinny. Why then, did she seem to make so much sense? I was lulled by her promises to take care of me. She alone could give me control over my anxiety, my body ... my life. Anna told me she had a plan. *"Trust me,"* she whispered, *"this plan is genius and it can't fail."*

It was at this critical moment that I heard mum bellow from downstairs. "Hally? ... Are you up?"

"Yes, Mum," I shouted from my bedroom.

"What's going on? You'll be late for school."

Anna said, *"Tell her you're not going to school."*

"I'm not going to school today, Mum."

"That's the first I've heard of it. I thought you were feeling better?"

Anna said, *"Tell her you're going to puke. That's no lie either."*

I said, "I feel a bit sick, Mum. I'm just gonna spend the morning in bed. Sorry. I'm not over the bug yet."

"It's your last week before the summer break, Hally. You've got your finals in 10 weeks' time."

Anna said, *"Like you'd forgotten. Your mother thinks you're a total idiot."*

I thought, 'She's just trying to help. She's coming upstairs ...'

Anna said, *"Quick! Get to the bathroom and stick your fingers down your throat. Now! We're staying home today. So we can thrash out our plan."* This was Anna's first order and for a crazy, fleeting moment, I considered resisting her. That was a mistake: a wave of anxiety swept me from my bed and carried me in the direction of the bathroom. I was so panicked that I kicked my bedside table, and hopped into the bathroom, an expression of stubbed-toe anguish on my face.

I locked the door.

Anna said, *"Crippling yourself was not part of the plan."* I grabbed my foot and began hopping up and down.

Anna said, *"Clumsy idiot!"*

Mum tapped on the door. "Are you all right in there? I thought I heard a squeal."

"I'll be fine. I just need to stay within barfing distance of the loo … go to work, Mum. I'll be okay … really."

"I'll call you later. Your mobile just beeped. You got a text."

I thought, 'Maybe it's Edward!?' I was about to make a bee-line for my mobile. Anna said, *"Take your hand off the door handle. Mother's still here."*

I let go of the handle and thought, 'I'm pretty sure I just heard the front door close.'

"We're not finished in here yet. You haven't weighed yourself."

'Oh, yeah.' I stepped onto the scales.

Anna said, *"I've never trusted electric scales. They're programmed to make people feel better about themselves. That way, fat people buy them again when they crush them. Whatever that readout says, it's a lie. You need to add at least ten pounds."*

I muttered, "I'm 8 stone 6 pounds."

Anna said, "9 *stone 3 it is then. That's the biggest you've ever been. No wonder Sophie said you're too fat to be a model. She wasn't wrong. Look in the mirror … if you can stomach it."*

I gazed into the bathroom mirror. "What's *wrong* with me?"

Anna said, *"You used to be thin, that's what's* wrong *with you. Jesus. You really do look like shit. No wonder Edward's been seeing Charlotte. Check out those roots, girl. They look like mousey sewage seeping through cheap blond highlights … and the less said about those bags under your eyes the better. We didn't really need the scales to tell us how gross you are these days, did we?"*

I burst into tears.

"Crying? Oh, that's really going to help. Oh, well. Go on. Knock yourself out. Make your eyes look like blue-bottles rotting in puff pastry again. It's not like you don't know why you're cracking up."

I sobbed, "E … Edward?"

"That's right. Edward. Your ever-expanding waist line. Oh, and let's not forget your fat ass."

I sobbed on, 'Mum said someone left me a message. It … it might be from Edward.'

"You sob that like it's a good thing? If it wasn't for the worry that guy has caused, you'd never have become so miserable."

I straightened myself and adopted my former resolve. I thought, 'That's a bit harsh. Anyway, Edward loves me.'

Anna was quick to set me straight on this. She said, *"Did he stick up for you when Sophie said what everyone was thinking?"*

'That I'm too fat to model? Well, no but … '

"But nothing. He actually smirked."

'I can't help how I feel about him.'

"Maybe. But right now, he thinks you're a joke. A big, fat, joke. Why else would he have started screwing Charlotte? Your nose is running. It's disgusting. Blow it."

I blew my nose and limped into my bedroom. I picked up my mobile and discovered the text was from Edward. It said, 'Call me Babe'.

Anna said, *"Wasn't Babe the name of the pig in that DVD he made you sit through last summer?"*

I murmured, "Oh, give me a break."

"Don't kid yourself. What are you doing?"

'… I'm calling him back.'

Anna said, *"Are you crazy? If you want him to like you, you need to think this through. Put down the phone."*

'But if I don't call him back, he'll hate me.'

"Wake-up call. He already hates you. And the only way to stop feeling this way, to get some control over your life, is to focus on you. You're doing well. You haven't eaten in 24 hours. And you're feeling a bit better about yourself ..."

'That's true. But I'm so hungry.'

Anna reassured me. *"You'll get used to hunger. You'll see it as a sign that you're heading in the right direction. When you weigh yourself tomorrow, you'll have achieved something ... and you'll feel less of a failure for once."*

Just then, my mobile started vibrating in my hand. I fumbled, dropped it, and yelled, "For God's sake!"

Anna said, "*Don't even* think *about answering it.*"

'But it might not even *be* him.'

I sat on the edge of my bed and called voice mail. Edward's voice, "Hi Babe. Why no show today? I thought you'd beaten the lurgy? Anyway, listen, my parents are out all evening. Come round at 7 … can't wait to see you."

Anna said, "*You've been summoned. He's treating you like a total slut. As usual.*"

'… I shouldn't go. Should I?'

"*What? And let him fumble his way through all your new layers of fat? 'Cos that would make so much sense.*"

'I'll call and tell him I'm ill.'

"*Better not. You'll just sound like some lying freak. Best switch off your phone.*"

Chapter 2

Several days later. Midnight.

Anna hadn't spoken in over an hour. I reasoned she must be sleeping. Since day one, the idea of Anna being a *separate* voice, lurking in my mind, seemed pretty obvious. It seems to me that our heads are full of little voices. I'm not talking about being schitzo, that's when people literally *hear* voices. These voices are internal. And they're harmless. It's like when you can't decide whether to wear the blue jeans or the black ones. There will be this one voice that puts all the reasons why you should go with the blue jeans, "*They make your ass look smaller, they're not as tight around the crotch,* and *they match your new belt.*" So anyway, you're about to reach for the blue jeans when this *other* voice says, "*Wait up, Dummy! You should wear the black jeans 'cos you wore the blue ones like a* dozen times *already. People will think they're the only jeans you have. And they probably stink. Smell 'em and see.*" Anyway, the longer it takes us to weigh up two sides of an argument, the more draining it is. And if you *can't* decide what to wear, you'll start tearing your hair out. Most of these voices are friendly and useful, whereas other voices can be a real pain in the ass, and remind us about the stuff we'd rather forget. It's like all these voices have their own files or something. For instance, before Anna arrived, the voice that reminded me of Edward was the most talkative in my mind. Man, the time I spent wallowing in Edward's file, scrutinising him – his looks, the things he said, the way he made me feel. Well, since Anna had stormed my head, Edward's voice had struggled for a look-in. I folded my arms, smiled and muttered, "What of that boy? I so wish he were here right now." Anna didn't trust Edward one bit and, if she'd been listening, she would have had something to say about that. I closed my eyes and anticipated her setting the record straight. Not a peep. I reasoned she couldn't be listening. So, feeling like a naughty child left alone with the cookie jar, I opened Edward's 'file' and had a rummage. At first, my recollections were delightful: our first kiss, our first night together, the warmth of his body. It was all so yummy and comforting and, for several minutes, I felt giddy with happiness. Then I stumbled into the painful stuff. Charlotte was the star of this grisly parade of memories and imaginings. Shameless and unremorseful, she winked at me and jumped into bed with Edward. Jealousy clawed at my insides. I got myself out of Edward's file by focusing on a sliver of light on my bedroom ceiling. It looked like a luminous exclamation mark. I gazed up and tried desperately to anchor myself to it. "Anna's right. I should try not to think about Edward." I leapt from my bed and marched, as though in a strop, towards the bathroom, wiping tears from my cheeks. I splashed cold water on my face and somehow resisted the urge to look in the mirror.

Anna had warned me about raking this stuff up. Once again, she was right. I grabbed my bath towel and slumped to the floor. I wrapped the towel around myself for warmth. The fact was, apart from the hunger, I'd felt a whole lot better for following Anna's advice. I huddled inside the towel and thought about how understanding mum and dad had been since Anna arrived. They were convinced all this had been caused by a flu virus. Dad had brought a tray of food up to my room at tea-time. After he'd left, I sat and stared at the plate of steamed vegetables. I guess having food in my room was making me nauseous, so I took Anna's advice and flushed it down the toilet.

At 4am, I got off the bathroom floor and returned to bed. I gazed up at the little exclamation mark of light. My mind projected a single word before it: FOOD! Now Anna was asleep, the idea of eating a little didn't fill me with dread. I thought, 'Just a light snack? A yoghurt with some friendly bacteria, perhaps?'

I headed for the kitchen.

It's always been cold in our kitchen at night. It felt doubly so on that night. To make matters worse, the neighbour's dog was barking at something in their yard. I whispered, "Shut up, mutt. You might wake Anna." My eyes opened wide. "Maybe the dog's trying to warn me *about* Anna." I was so hungry I was willing to take that chance. Mum always kept the fridge stacked with pots of low-fat yoghurt. Apple and cinnamon sounded good. It tasted even better. Then I tucked into some corn flakes with a splash of milk. I pushed the cereal bowl to one side and spotted the fruit bowl. That damn fruit bowl had been the centre-piece of our kitchen table for as long as I could remember. It looked like a still-life painting in that sombre light. A banana sat on top like a yellow emergency handle. It seemed to say 'Pull me!' I thought, 'Okay. But no more.'

I crept back into bed. Turned onto my side and thought, 'I'm such an idiot! I've eaten too much! It's heading straight for my hips.'

Anna loomed from the shadows. *"That's right … your hips, your thighs, your ass, your stomach, your legs. What were you thinking?"*

I thought, 'I don't know. I was just so hungry.'

Anna said, *"Don't you get it? Don't you see? Hunger is your new guide. It's the one thing that can lead you in the right direction: happiness. Hunger is gobbling up your fat, your confusion, your anxiety."* The next instant, it felt as though a trap-door had opened beneath me. This is what happens when the trap-door opens. My chest tightens to BURSTING point; my heart bangs like a manic drum, I can't breathe, and I'm convinced I'm going to die. I thought, 'Anna please! Help me! I'm sorry! I think I'm *dying*!'

Anna said, *"It's not that easy. It's about choices. If you make the right choices, I can protect you. Make the wrong choices and …"*

I wheezed, "Yes … yes … must make the right choices … I did a really stupid thing … but it won't … won't happen again …' As I lay clutching at my heart, my anxiety attack began to fade.

Chapter 3

The following morning, I was woken by the landline. My eyes fluttered open. "Edward?!" Mum was coming upstairs. I thought, 'Oh God, she's *talking* to someone.' The trap-door creaked and groaned. Mum tapped on my bedroom door. I turned towards the wall and closed my eyes.

"Are you awake, Hally? Sophie's on the phone … she wants to know how you are. You haven't replied to her texts …"

I thought, 'It's just Soph!' and called out, "One sec, Mum."

I climbed out of bed and opened the door.

Mum was wearing a dressing-gown. We were nose-to-nose. Her brow furrowed. "You look awful, darling."

I thanked Mum for her observation and closed the door. I opened the door again and took the phone. "Hi, Soph."

Soph said, "Hey, what's going on? Are you okay? What's the deal with your mobile?"

Anna loomed from the shadows. "*Tell her you've lost the charger.*"

I said, "I can't find the charger …"

Soph said, "So, you're still fighting the flu?"

"It's totally zapped my energy."

An awkward silence. Then Soph said, "Are you pissed off with me, Hally?"

I said, "Pissed off? With you? No. Why?"

Soph said, "I honestly didn't mean to upset you the other day."

Sounding none-the-wiser, I asked, "What do you mean?"

Soph said, "You looked at me strangely … when I said you'd probably need to lose some weight, you know, if you were *actually* going to do some modelling. Which you would *never do*."

Anna said, "*No harm done.*"

I thought, 'Anna's a comedian.'

I said, "What? No. I'm fine about that. Anyway, you were right."

Soph said, "Listen Babe, I've had Edward onto me. He sent me a text first thing. I just called him back and he's worried because you haven't returned his calls. He thinks you're dumping him, Hally."

I said, "Dumping *him*? Why would he care? He's got Char …"

Anna butted in. *"Don't mention her. Soph won't understand. She'll just think you're being paranoid."*

Soph said, "You're not worried about *Charlotte Smith*? That's so ridiculous!"

Anna said, *"Oh,* well *done. Now she thinks you're ridiculous. You have to get off this phone. Tell her you have to go. You're going to puke."*

I said, "Sorry, Soph. I gotta go. I think I'm going to hurl." I took the phone out onto the landing and placed it on the table. I returned to my room, closed the door and thought, 'Soph thinks I'm just being paranoid about Edward and Charlotte. Maybe I am?'

Anna said, *"Maybe you should think again. What does she know about anything? You know what you saw. And not just you, others have seen them."*

I took a deep breath, crossed the room and sat on the edge of my bed. I thought, 'They were only *talking* when I saw them…'

Anna said, *"But they stopped talking real fast the second they saw you. Well, didn't they?"*

I thought, 'I suppose so, but …'

Anna said, *"And they looked completely guilty?"*

I thought, 'That's true, they really did, but …'

Anna said, *"They looked so into each other. It's obvious he really fancies her. What guy wouldn't? She's still gorgeous."*

I thought, 'Yes … but maybe Sophie *was* right? Maybe I am just being paranoid?' Damn it! I'm going to call him right now ...'

The trap-door flew open beneath me. I wheezed, "What's … happening … to … me!"

Anna said, *"This is your fault. Why don't you listen to me?"*

I thought, 'I'm so confused! I don't know what to do or think!'

Anna made a suggestion. She said, *"Why don't you weigh yourself?"*

I thought, 'Yes! Maybe that will help.'

Anna was so reassuring. She said, *"Who knows, maybe you've lost a few pounds? If you have, I might be able to pull you out of there ... and shore up the trap-door."* With heart pounding, breath racing, and butterflies gnawing, I stumbled into the bathroom. I stood on the scales and prayed that I'd lost some weight. There was a delay as the little red lights flickered on and did their customary march to the right. Then the display read: 8 stone 4 pounds.

I made fists and thought, 'I've lost 3lb!'

Anna said, *"Well done! See? You're not a total waste of space after all. How do you feel?"*

Right then, my anxiety attack was swept away by a feeling of euphoria. Like I'd just won the lottery. I thought, 'I feel great! I should call Soph back and tell her the fab news.'

Anna said, *"Are you sure that's wise?"*

I thought, 'Sophie's cool. I mean, it was her idea to lose some weight in the first place.'

Mum tapped on my bedroom door. She said, "Hally? Sophie's back on the phone."

I thought, 'I'll have to speak to her now.'

Anna remained silent.

I opened my bedroom door. Again mum studied my face. "You're as pale as a ghost, Hally."

I rolled my eyes, grabbed the phone and closed the door.

I said, "Hey, Soph!"

Soph said, "You sound better. You must have spoken to Edward?"

I announced, "I've lost another 3lbs!"

Soph said, "Oh, cool. How'd you manage that so quickly?"

My mind went blank.

Anna said, *"Blame the bug."*

I said, "The flu ... I haven't been able to keep anything down for days."

Soph giggled. "Maybe we should all catch it."

"I'm feeling so much better. What's going on later?"

"I'm going into town. Dad's given me some cash ... I'm desperate for some new pumps ... you feeling well enough for a shopping trip?"

"Absolutely! I haven't been out in over a week. I'm going nuts."

Another awkward silence. Then Soph said, "Shall we say Sloane Square? 12.30?"

"Perfect!"

I opened my closet door. My mind was a total blank until Anna said, *"None of this stuff does you any favours."*

I shrugged, reached in, and pulled out a pair of black jeans. 'These will just have to do. Anyway, they're pretty high-waisted.'

Anna said, *"Good choice. They'll hide your stomach. But expect a struggle getting them over those thighs."*

I thought, 'Oh, don't I know it. The last time I wore them I practically injured myself … but … hey, that wasn't so bad!' I thought, pulling up the zipper.

Anna found some kind words. She said, *"Reward for losing 3lbs?"*

I thought, '… I guess!'

Anna said, *"Better check your ass in the mirror."*

I turned, gazed over my shoulder.

Anna said, *"You've still got a long way to go, girl."*

I thought, 'No shit. Now which T-shirt should I wear?'

Anna advised, *"Nothing too tight …"*

I thought, ' Obviously … black's good … how about this one?'

Anna said, *"It's all right. But what about the black sweatshirt?"*

I thought, 'It's hot out. I'll bake in that.'

Anna said, 'It'll cover a multitude of sins though…'

I was still on my accomplishment high. So I stood my ground and thought, 'No. I really think this one will be okay.'

Anna said, *"Don't say I didn't warn you."*

I glided down the stairs and practically skipped into the kitchen. Mum was arranging the fruit bowl on the kitchen table. She asked me if I was feeling better. I was about to say, "Much better!"

Anna said, *"Idiot! You'll blow your stomach-bug cover!"*

I visibly deflated. "I'm feeling a little better, thanks …"

Mum said, "Are you going somewhere?"

"I'm just meeting Soph. I need to get out. Get some fresh air."

"What about breakfast?"

"I'd rather not risk it … upsetting my stomach."

"I can give you a lift to the station if you like?"

I nodded and left the kitchen.

Chapter 4

The District (underground) Line. Southfields to Sloane Square. Eight stops. It should have taken fifteen minutes. It had already been twenty five and we were stalled at Earls Court Station. It was sweltering and I could feel my T-shirt moistening and bonding with the harsh fabric of the seat. It felt gross, like hundreds of prickly suckers trying to fuse me to my clothing. The train's doors were open and the ventilation was welcome but our compartment was gradually filling with sweaty bodies. This meant less room and more unsavoury smells and I was beginning to feel claustrophobic.

Opposite me, an attractive black woman was sitting in a floral dress. She was an ample girl and I admired her courage for choosing not only the style but also the silken fabric. The garment was struggling to contain her and failing – her bust over-flowing from it like a fondue of dark flesh. I thought, 'Do guys really find that much flesh attractive?' I reasoned that if the guy standing over us was anything to go by – yes! The man in his pin-striped suit was clearly impressed. He was trying to read his newspaper; something on the page was interesting but not *as* interesting.

Anna said, *"The guy's a letch and a perv."*

I thought, 'You think so?'

Anna said, *"Who else but a sick perv would want to ogle that blubber? He's clearly not interested in you, though. Which is interesting."*

I thought, 'I'm probably not his type. Anyway, the blond guy sitting next to her has been checking me out … and he's actually rather cute. See. He just did it again.'

Anna said, *"Just because a guy looks at you doesn't mean he fancies you. Maybe you remind him of someone? He's probably been comparing you with his girlfriend and has reached the conclusion that you're a similar yet fatter version."*

The guy glanced at me again and then looked down at his fingers. Anna said, *"He's counting his blessings ... thinking how lucky he is to be going out with the thin version."*

I muttered, "For God's sake."

Anna said, "*Brilliant. Now he sees a fat girl who talks to herself.*" The guy smiled at me. But now he just made me feel uncomfortable, so I hugged my bag and looked away.

The train pulled into Sloane Square Station. I was thirty minutes late. I rode the escalator up past posters advertising shoes, make-up, video games ...

When I reached the top, I couldn't see Soph anywhere. There were plenty of people standing inside the station's entrance and outside on the pavement, mostly huddled conspiratorially in groups of twos and threes. Anna said, "*This is why you should avoid this place. Too many thin, gorgeous people.*"

I thought, 'People did used to say I should model.'

Anna said, "*You were fourteen then and they were mental.*" I suddenly felt horribly self-conscious and I couldn't see Soph anywhere. It's not like she'd be hard to miss with her jet black hair and willowy physique. Anna mumbled, '*Bitch.*'

I thought, 'But she isn't. Not really. I love Soph.' My nose began to twitch. I thought, '... I recognise that aftershave.'

A male voice behind me, unmistakably Edward's said, "Hally?"

I muttered, "Holy crap!"

Anna said, "*Don't turn around! Walk off and cross that road like you didn't hear him.*"

I thought, 'I can't do that! I'll look ridiculous. And anyway, the lights are green!'

"*Take a chance!*"

I turned and almost tripped over myself.

Anna said, "*Clown!*"

I said, "Edward! Hi! What are ...?"

Edward interrupted me with some well-rehearsed words of reassurance. He said, "It's okay, Babe, I'm not stalking you. I'm meeting John. Soph said you were meeting her here and ..." He adopted his most vulnerable, puppy dog expression. "I've missed you. What's going on? Are you pissed off with me? Have I done something?"

I thought, 'God. He looks so innocent.' He also looked seriously fit in his designer jeans and tight Nike T-shirt. He took a step forwards and put his arms around me.

Anna cried, "*Watch out! He's going to grab your FAT ass*!" Edward's fingers plunged into my fat ass, right down to the bone. I stepped back and shoved him away.

He said, "*Babe*, what's wrong? Why can't I hug my girl?"

I gaped at him. Like a fat fish out of water.

Anna said, "*Stupid girl. Blame the bug.*"

I said, "... I'm infected, Edward. My bug. I don't want you to catch it."

Edward took a deep breath. "Sophie said something about Charlotte? You don't actually think …"

I spluttered, "*What*? Whatever … I'm not your keeper."

"My *keeper*? … I've bumped into her a couple of times … we're friends. I only want you!"

He stepped forwards and was about to put his hands on my waist. Anna said, "*Reverse gear!*"

I took a backward step. "Edward … please! Don't."

"You're really cutting me up, Hally. Look, at least come and get a coffee. Please."

"… You know I can't. I'm meeting Soph."

"She'll call when she gets here."

"I didn't bring my phone."

Edward smiled. "I brought mine."

I thought, 'That smile. I can't resist it ...'

Anna said, "*You'll live to regret this.*"

The Oriel is a wine bar come brasserie. As we walked in, Anna said, "*You never have liked this place. Always did find it too pretentious and up its own ass. All this dark wood, brass, stick-thin waitresses and beautiful people. You're already starting to feel uncomfortable.*" I caught myself nodding in agreement. The hostess came over and smiled at me like I was some kind of nodding freak. She led us to a table *right* in the middle of the place.

Anna said, "*Oh, the perfect position. Now everyone's going to see how fat and out of place you are.*" I sat down. Anna suggested that I slouch. So I did.

Edward placed his elbows on the table, leaned forward and said, "Hally, you've been crying … I can always tell 'cos your eyes … they go greener." Then he sat back and raised an eyebrow. "Something's different about you, Babe … where's that feisty hot-headed chick I fell for?"

I smiled for the first time. "*Different*? Do you think so? I have lost a few pounds." He didn't reply and started fiddling with his watch strap. I thought, 'He looks so sad. Are those *tears* ...?'

He said, "Are you going to finish with me, Hally?"

Anna said, "*Just tell him yes. Let's get this farce over with.*"

I said, "... Look, I'm going through some stuff ... I just need some space ... I've been feeling like ... like I'm getting ..."

Anna said, "*If you mention your weight he'll never understand. He'll just think you're nuts.*"

Edward said, "Feeling like *what*, Babe?"

I said, "Don't call me that. *Please*. I'm not a Babe."

Edward shook his head. "You're not making any sense ..."

He reached across the table, grabbed my hands and said, "What is it? Talk to me. *Please*."

Anna said, "*Say nothing. And break eye contact.*"

I looked around the room.

Edward said, "... Hally, we've been seeing each other for 6 months ... but ... it feels like so much longer than that."

I muttered, "Thanks a bunch."

Edward caressed my fingers. "You know what I mean."

Our waitress loomed over us. She *had* to be the thinnest waitress in London. To make matters worse, she had a sexy French accent. I looked at Edward to see if he'd noticed how gorgeous she was. He looked up at the waitress. "I'll have a cappuccino and ... I'd really love one of your muffins."

Anna said, "*He's flirting with her. She obviously doesn't mind. Now they're both looking at you ... I suggest you say something, Dummy.*"

I said, "I'd like ..."

Anna said, "*Did you see that? The bitch just looked at your body and practically rolled her eyes in disgust.*"

I cleared my throat and continued, "... a mineral water."

The waitress asked, "Nothing to eat?"

I shook my head. Sophie approached from behind me. She said, "I had a feeling I'd find you guys here."

Subtlety had never been Sophie's strong point. And for several excruciating minutes, she prodded and probed Edward and I using sly glances, innuendos and borderline sarcastic comments. I thought, 'Bless her. She's just trying to help. But I can't smile awkwardly for much longer. My cheeks are numb.' They stumbled into another subject: revision. They'd both done a fair bit.

Edward said, "I would have done more … but I've had a lot on my mind." He looked at me.

Anna said, *"Emotional blackmail? That's low, even from a cheating scumbag like him."*

Sophie asked me if I'd managed to get any revision done. All I could think was, 'I'm really starting to feel like crap. Why do I feel so emotional?'

Anna said, *"You're going to burst into tears … excuse yourself and go to the ladies."*

I stood up and said, "I'll be back in a tick, guys."

Edward asked, "Are you okay?"

"I'm fine."

Soph said, "You look very pale all of a sudden. Are you sure you're okay?"

I nodded and walked away.

Anna said, *"God! Why do they have to ask so many questions?"*

I pushed open the bathroom door, went inside and thought, 'They're just concerned about me.'

Anna said, *"They're just damn nosey. The first cubicle is free. It doesn't look too disgusting. Lock the door."* I locked the door and sat down. Anna said, *"On a scale of 1-10, how FAT and WORTHLESS are you feeling right now?"*

I thought, 'Make that a 10.'

Anna said, *"There's a tissue in your pocket."*

I blew my nose and burst into tears.

Anna said, *"Someone's come in! Keep the sobbing down. It might be Soph."*

I thought, 'At least Edward *seems* to still like me.'

Anna said, *"Oh, God. You didn't buy into all that crap did you? Guys only care about their egos. They're selfish pricks. If you dumped him his ego would never live it down. That's the only reason he's being 'nice.' He's buttering you up … so he can dump you in a couple of weeks."* I blew my nose again. Anna said, *"We can't stay in here forever; pull yourself together and then go back out there and tell them you're feeling ill. Then bolt for the tube."* It sounded like the perfect plan.

Chapter 5

It had been six weeks since Anna's arrival. I'd lost nine pounds. Since week four, I'd been surviving on something I'd spotted on the cover of 'What Diet Monthly Magazine?' called 'The Lemonade Diet.' The glossy blue and red banner boasted that you could 'lose pounds and replace energy.' Anna said, *"It sounds ideal … and it might even stop you whining about having no energy."*

The ingredients of the diet were simple: a glass of lemonade, a squirt of maple syrup and a sprinkling of pepper. Hey presto! You had a concoction with few calories that gave you an energy boost.

Edward had tried to call me several times since I'd made my hasty exit from the Oriel. I told mother to say I was out. Sophie realised I needed some space. But she also knew I was going through some stuff. I guess she was pissed off because I hadn't confided in her.

I'd been existing in my own little world, with mainly Anna for company. I felt muddled. A lack of carbs and protein will do that. And the more muddled I became the more it felt like I *needed* Anna's guidance. It was around this time that she suggested I visit a pro ana website. I had read about these so called 'support groups' a couple of years back. At that time, I remember how shocked I was at the idea of young people encouraging one another to starve. The article I read was upsetting. But now, the idea of visiting a pro ana site and talking with other girls who had their own Annas was enticing. I typed 'pro ana' into Google and clicked on the third entry from the top. I was confronted by a list of personal entries, each with its own little picture representing the owner. Some girls had chosen famous anorexics to represent them, some cartoon characters. Others had fashioned glimpses of body-parts; like hands or feet or belly buttons. My eyes quickly came to rest on Munch's 'Scream.' The little square containing the panicked character grasping his head made perfect sense. I clicked on the picture to see what 'Tammy' had to say for herself. This is what Tammy said:

Hi guys! I'm back. They finally let me out of hospital after 2 weeks of tube feeding HELL. They fattened me up good this time. Man, I'm over 6 stone again. Those bastards pumped 12 pounds of gook into my body. I thought America was supposed to be the land of the free??? What a joke. Anyway, I'm out now and back on track. What's new with you guys?

Tammy.

I recoiled from the computer and paced up and down my room – images of feeding tubes and doctors in white coats hot on my heels. I thought, 'Is that the fate that awaits me?'

Anna said, "*We're cleverer than that. They'll never figure it out.*"

'That's probably just what Tammy thought!'

Anna said, "*Anyway, she's fine now. Said she's back on track. So no harm done.*"

'No harm *done*? She was probably sectioned like some nutter.'

Anna made a suggestion. She said, "*Why don't you send her a message? Ask her where she went wrong?*"

So I did. And I wrote:

Hi Tammy,

I'm Hally. I've only known Anna for six weeks but I've lost 9lbs. I read your message and it frightened me. It sounds like they have put you through hell. I don't like hospitals. Can you give me any tips on avoiding them??? I'm feeling so isolated right now. It's mainly just Anna and me. My parents are still buying a flu virus story. I don't know how much time I have before they get suspicious. In desperate need of reassurance! Hally x

I decided to have a look around the same site and came across a posting from someone without an eating disorder. She claimed to be doing some research into the 'illness' and had left 5 questions that she hoped would be answered by anorexics.

The questions were pretty basic:

How long have you had anorexia?

How much weight have you lost?

What do you see when you look in the mirror?

Why do you visit pro ana sites?

How do you see your life ending up?

Several people had tried to answer her questions as best they could. However, the response that captured my attention was one that contained a tirade of hate-filled venom. It read: Get lost loser! You are NOT welcome here. This is our site! And we're not freaks! You're the freak BITCH. Go and find some place else to stick your fat bitch nose in.

I wondered if this girl's rant had been dictated by her own Anna. I wondered what she had been like *before* Anna. Then I had a truly horrifying thought – what if this girl could no longer tell the difference between her own thoughts and Anna's voice? Might Anna take her over completely? If that happened, she would *become* Anna. I muttered, "Could *I* become Anna?"

Anna shuffled in a darkened corner of my mind. She said, "*That's ridiculous. You're losing the plot.*" A knock on my bedroom door startled me. My little sis walked in. I lowered the lid of my laptop.

Sarah planted herself on the end of my bed. She said, "What are you doing?"

I rubbed my neck and said, "Nothing. Just checking my emails."

She said, "You're acting all suspicious."

I tried to claw back the adult high ground. "You mean I'm acting *suspiciously*."

She said, "Whatever. You're up to something. I can tell."

"I've had a serious flu bug. It made me very sick." I patted my stomach and tried to look even more pathetic than I already felt.

She said, "That was ages ago." Then she lifted the lid of my laptop ... "Who's *Ana*?"

I closed it again, slowly. "None of your business. Now scram!" I tickled her and chased her out of the room. My head *spun* and I collapsed at the base of the door. I sat there watching stars. Then I got into bed and closed my eyes.

Suddenly, mum's standing over me. "Is everything okay? It's not like you to sleep in the middle of the afternoon."

I sat up, yawned and said, "This plague thing can linger for months, Mum."

"How about I make you some broth?"

Anna said, "*Just say yes. You can flush it.*"

I said, "That actually sounds really good, Mum. Thanks."

Anna said, "*Check your emails. Maybe Tammy's replied?*"

I thought, 'Oh yeah!' and switched on my laptop.

I did have a message from Tammy, it read:

Congratulations on losing 9lbs! I know what you're saying about hospitals. I hate 'em too. As my shrink pointed out, 'If you don't like hospitals Tammy, don't go giving yourself a heart attack at 15.' Like I choose to have a heart attack! It's not my fault my folks and their folks had lame hearts. Take comfort girl, I was the exception not the rule! Keep in touch now. I'm here to help if I can. T xx

Anna said, "*See? You had that melt-down for nothing. The girl has a dodgy heart. It would have landed her in hospital, no matter what.*"

I thought, 'Maybe she never would've had a heart attack in the first place … if she hadn't been starving herself.'

Anna said, "*What, you're a doctor now? As well as a fat failure?*"

The next day, I left Tammy another message. She replied and suggested we meet in a private chat room. I keyed in the password Tammy gave me. I heard a 'ping' and the following text appeared.

Tammy wrote: Hi Hally. Hope I didn't keep you waiting?

I wrote: No, I Just got here. How are things?

Tammy wrote: The pressure's really on right now. But when is it ever off???

I wrote: Please tell more …

Tammy wrote: Are you sure you wanna know?!?

I wrote: I need to know.

Tammy wrote: I had a heart murmur yesterday and passed out in the yard in front of a neighbour. I landed on some old lady's rose bush and scratched up my arm real bad.

I wrote: Did they take you to hospital?

Tammy wrote: Of course. Any excuse.

I wrote: But they let you out?

Tammy wrote: Oh yeah. A victory for our team! They couldn't keep me in cos I've maintained my weight.

I wrote: So you've been eating more?

Tammy wrote: No way! I dunno what the deal is. It happens sometimes. I guess I just got lucky. But I convinced em! Told em I'd been sticking to their calorie intake sheet.

I wrote: They must have believed you. Anna's such a help when it comes to lying.

Tammy wrote: Anna???

I wrote: Anna. The voice in our head. You know *Anna* … Anna Rexia.

Tammy wrote: I never really thought about it like that. That's actually pretty cute.

It stunned me that Tammy didn't 'get' Anna the way I did. But I didn't let on. I wrote: Your parents must be so worried about you.

Tammy wrote: It's not like I don't feel guilty about that. But what can I do? You know the deal.

I wrote: I know. I feel like I've got a trap-door under me 24/7. Waiting to plunge me into all kinds of hell if I make a wrong move.

Tammy wrote: I get that. I really do.

I wrote: Anna helps me keep the trap-door closed. That's why it's important to listen to her. Not take her for granted.

Tammy wrote: God, yes! Are you like some kind of shrink or something??

I wrote: No way! It's just how I see things. How long has Anna been taking care of you?

Tammy wrote: Since I was 12. I'm gonna be 15 next month.

I wrote: *That* long?????

Tammy wrote: Yep. I've been in hospital 8 times. Can you believe that? As soon as I get down to a weight that makes me happy, they stick a tube in me.

I wrote: They probably saved your life.

Tammy wrote: Well, I just wish they'd leave me the hell alone. How are you doing?

I wrote: Early days. Nobody suspects. But I'm terrified about letting people down.

Tammy wrote: It's not like 'Anna' gives us a choice.

I wrote: It helps so much having someone besides Anna to talk to. Can we meet in this room again sometime?

Tammy wrote: Sure thing girlfriend!

Chapter 6

My third month with Anna had been a repetition of the first two. Only now I was pretending to have stomach troubles. My waking hours consisted of these four activities: weighing myself, looking at myself, deceiving myself (and others obviously) and avoiding food. What made my deceitfulness all the more shocking was that, until Anna, I'd been such a terrible liar. Honest to God! More often than not, I'd be betrayed by a hot flush that left me red, flustered and looking as guilty as hell. But not now. Now I had my own personal tutor in the art of deceit, and Anna was the best in the business. Lying had become a breeze with her pre-empting any tricky questions or situations. It's strange to think how Anna is a part of me. She lives inside my mind, so how could she be so different? So skilled at deception when I had been so useless? At that time, this was something I couldn't fathom.

For someone suffering with acute insecurity, I was also spending a ridiculous amount of time staring at myself in mirrors. I was five feet nine tall, weighed 7st 2lbs, and felt fat. You probably think I was delusional and seeing some distorted view, like I was looking in a fairground mirror. But that's not the case. I didn't think I LOOKED fat at all. I FELT fat. How could this be when I was looking more and more skeletal? Well, it's like, even though I couldn't SEE the fat on my body, I could FEEL the fat on my body. In the same way you might have felt lonely. Or felt stupid. Or felt jealous. Or felt let down. Or felt horny. I felt fat. I also got this weird tingling in my body sometimes. It felt like my body was a life-jacket being inflated. Only there was no life jacket, just my vanishing body.

Edward hadn't tried to call me in a while. To be honest, I was feeling too tired to care. Emotions require energy and I'd never realised *how much* energy until Anna gate-crashed the party.

My weight loss had slowed down a bit. This has something to do with the body compensating for the lack of nutrients by slowing down the metabolism – which makes you feel sluggish on top of everything else. My 'menu,' which had been approved by Anna, was short. It consisted of 'The Lemonade Diet' for breakfast (one glass) and a shallow bowl of watercress soup for lunch. Occasionally, I was allowed a rice cracker before bed. I'd avoided sit-down meals with the family by preparing 'show meals' in the kitchen. I would carry them upstairs on a tray. Anything that wasn't on the 'menu' was flushed.

Not long after, I was taken far from the comfort zone of my bedroom and into a situation that would test Anna's powers of deception to their very limits ...

Chapter 7

It was a Saturday and my cousin Verity was getting married. Her father threw his only daughter a no-expense-spared bash at a swanky hotel. The flu virus excuse had run its course and I needed to keep my wits around food. In the dictionary of My Life, under 'wits' it said, 'see Anna'. I'd lost 17lb and, at the time, it felt like *such* an accomplishment. As regards arousing suspicion, things were about to come to a head at home. I'd dropped 4 dress sizes and my wedding frock threatened to engulf me in a marquee of purple and black. I stared at myself in the mirror and thought, 'Oh, crap ... I look like a walking tent pole.'

My sister rustled through my bedroom door in her maid of honour's outfit. She said, "Well? How gorgeous am I?"

I said, "You look great, sis."

She gazed at me. I could see the cogs turning and providing her mind with a selection of possible comments concerning her shrinking sister. She settled on, "You look terrible. You need to eat something."

Anna said, "*All right!*"

I smiled.

Mum entered my room. She was fiddling with her pearl necklace. She looked up and said, "Bloody Hell. It's the incredible shrinking daughter!" My father was passing on the landing and must have heard her. He joined the assembled party. My family stood and gawped at me.

I said, "Do you mind? I've lost some weight. I have been ill, you know."

Dad straightened his black tie, nervously cleared his throat and said, "*Ill*? I'll say. We should have put you in quarantine."

Sarah said, "Quarantine? Has she got rabies then?"

Dad ruffled Sarah's hair, "Has she bitten anyone recently?"

Sarah nodded enthusiastically. "Probably."

Mother pulled in my dress at the back. She said, "Sarah, get my sewing kit, would you? It's in my dressing table. Third drawer down on the left." She twirled me around so I was facing the mirror, grabbed a fistful of fabric and said, 'We might just be able to get away with it … you'll have to keep your cardi on ...'"

I was relieved that she didn't suspect anything beyond the virus. I said, "Sounds like a good plan, Mum."

First stop, the church.

I slid out of the car and stood six feet tall in my heels. I felt indescribably proud that I'd reached the coveted size zero. My family might be clueless heathens but, to the outside world, I would be the envy of one and all. A gaggle of relatives were mingling on the steps of the church. Our little herd approached the group.

What followed was the usual parade of smiling, inquisitive heads. I know it's a cliché but I really *had* grown taller since these people had seen me last. We're talking over a foot. But doesn't the contrast go both ways? To my eyes, many of my relatives had *shrunk*. But did I bring this up? No, I did not. I responded politely to the following questions and statements of the obvious:

Aunt Sheila said, "My, you've grown, Hally!"

A third cousin, once removed, with a white beard asked, "What have they been feeding you on?"

I muttered, "Rice cakes and lemonade."

"Really? So what's the weather like up there anyway?"

I adjusted my cardi, smiled and muttered, "It pisses down most days."

Not a single comment had been made about my considerable achievement. This was more than a little irksome and I wanted to rip off my cardi and show them. Anna advised me to wait until the evening for the grand unveiling.

The bride arrived fashionably late and looked amazing. She'd obviously been on a strict diet in preparation for her big day. She must have sacrificed a *lot* to fit into her dress. Unbelievably, I overheard a poisonous comment. My Uncle John said, "She's nothing but skin and bone. It's not healthy. I blame those damn women's magazines."

I negotiated my way around his considerable girth, patted his bulging belly and said, "And this *is* healthy, is it?"

He smiled awkwardly. "I've worked hard on that. It's prime northern beef, is that."

I glanced at the bride and said, "I know which look I prefer."

He said, "You're all the same you southern lasses – nothing but skin and bone yourself."

Anna said, "*He paid you a compliment!*"

I said, "Cheers, Uncle John! Do you really think so?"

Uncle John chuckled nervously and moved away.

The reception was pretty grand. Four hundred guests, all allocated seats in the hotel's ballroom. The first thing I did after locating my table was remove my cardi. After all, why shouldn't I show off my new physique? People who go to the gym show off *their* muscles at every opportunity. I draped my cardi over the back of my chair and sat down; mother's alterations masked perfectly by its high-back. Seated to my right was my cousin George. George is 16. To my left was his sister Katie. Katie is 15. She has always enjoyed her food. To be perfectly frank, at 5'1" and 13 stone, she's pretty enormous. I felt like a fat stork sitting beside a hippo and wondered if she felt the same in reverse.

Anna made a fair comment. She said, "*If it wasn't for me, there would have been two hippos side-by-side at this table.*" I eye-balled the bread rolls with utter contempt. Meanwhile, Katie had lunged at them before her ass had hit her chair. Her chubby fingers, apparently set on automatic, plastered a knob of curly butter on the roll which disappeared into her gob before you could shout "Childhood obesity!"

She chewed, paused for thought, chewed some more, swallowed and said, "I'm *famished* after all that church stuff. Aren't you?" Then she glanced at me suspiciously.

I said, "No. Not really. I want to leave plenty of room for the coming feast."

Katie rolled her brown eyes, "I'm *supposed* to be on a diet. Mother will kill me if she sees me eating rolls. Bread is off the menu."

Her brother, a blushing boy with a blond quiff and acne said, "Apparently, she's got some kind of disease. Just can't help herself around food."

Katie looked at her brother like he was dumber than the bread roll she was eating. She said, "And anorexia *isn't* a disease?"

I shifted uneasily in my seat, "What do you mean? I'm not anorexic."

She said, "I never said you were. My, we are defensive aren't we?"

Anna said, *"We'll have to keep an eye on that one. She's a bright kid."*

At the table's centre, a silver vase erupted in a fountain of flowers and exotic fruits. Before us, four sets of knives, forks and spoons, polished to within an inch of their lives. This meant four waves of attack from the enemy.

The first course arrived: a selection of three different soups in three little bowls. I picked up my spoon, scooped up some broth and awaited instructions.

Anna said, *"This three bowl deal is to our advantage."*

I thought, '*Really*? How am I supposed to dispose of all this soup?' I blew on the tepid broth.

Anna said, *"... Pretend to sip some and then dump the soup on your spoon into the other bowls. Continue doing this until you've emptied one bowl. That will do for the first course."*

I thought. 'What about the nosey so-and-so to my right?'

Anna told me to look at her. I glanced to my right and grimaced at the sight of Katie scoffing the first bowl. Anna said, *"Nothing but soup exists in her world right now."*

By the time Katie was scraping the bottom of her final bowl, I'd managed to empty one of mine into the other two. I sat back, and patted the sides of my clean mouth with my clean napkin. Katie gave her pronouncement on the soup: "Yum!"

She glanced at my *one* empty bowl and then sighed in disbelief at the other two. Anna suggested that I distract her. I said, "Have you got a boyfriend?"

"No."

On my left, her brother was now playing with a DS games machine. He said, "... That's 'cos he dumped her."

Katie said, "He didn't *dump* me! We came to an arrangement."

George said, "Yeah. He arranged to start seeing Debbie Swain."

Katie reached for another bread roll and said, "His loss."

The shy kid on my right was rapidly coming out of his shell. He said, "Are you seeing anyone, Hally?"

Katie said, "She's hardly going to be interested in a kid like you, is she?"

George said, "What's that got to do with anything. Anyway, why are you wasting time talking when you could be eating?"

Katie shrugged and bit into her roll. Between chews she said, "Are *you* seeing anyone, Hally?"

I didn't want to talk about Edward. Or think about him. I felt the trap-door creak at the very notion. "That subject's a bit raw, right now."

Katie said, "You broke up then?"

"No. It's just on hold at the moment. It's complicated."

The waiter whisked away our plates.

The next course was smoked salmon, on a plate with potato skins and cream cheese. Anna said, "*Shove the smoked salmon inside the potato skins. Then close the potato skins and bunch them up on the side of the plate.*" It seemed to work a treat. And I imagined no one had noticed.

The main course was a generous portion of salmon on a bed of rice and steamed vegetables. At this point, Katie's appetite provided the ideal solution. She said, "I love salmon. It's my favourite."

Anna said, "*Tell her you're allergic to seafood. She'll* want *to believe you.*"

Anna was so right about that. Katie forked my salmon and said, "Well, if you're sure?"

"Honestly, I'd break out in hives. So, be my guest." That only left a plate of vegetables and rice to dispose of. On Anna's advice, my hand shot to the side and dumped my glass of water over it. Some water splashed on George's DS. "Hey, watch out!"

I said, "God, I'm *so* clumsy!"

I excused myself and made good my escape to the ladies room.

Chapter 8

I gazed at myself in the rest-room's mirror. Powerful spotlights made my shoulder blades look sharp and pronounced. I thought, 'I'm becoming angular … like a white kite.' I was relieved by the sight of my chest bones, pushing into my flesh, and turning it red.

Anna said, "*Congratulations! You're the proud owner of a red carpet chest.*" I smiled at myself in the mirror. Just then the door opened. A tall brunette, wearing a black strapless gown, walked in. She smiled at me curiously and disappeared inside a cubicle. Anna said, "*Do you know her?*"

'I've never seen her before.' I turned so I could see my back in the mirror. Got an eyeful of mother's alterations. I thought, 'Oh, crap!' and fiddled about with them, trying to make them look less obvious. The woman flushed her toilet.

Anna said, "*Time to leave.*"

Anna suggested that I waste some time before returning to the table. I spotted an empty seat in the hotel's foyer and made a bee-line for it. The red armchair was large and comfy and it practically gobbled me up. I crossed my legs and started fiddling with the ends of my hair. Two dishy guys hurried past carrying a vacuum cleaner and a dustpan and brush. The taller one smiled at me. I blushed and smiled back. I continued to fiddle with my hair, checking for split ends. Then I felt eyes on me … and looked up. It was the woman from the rest-room, talking to an old lady but staring at *me*. But she wasn't smiling now – she looked concerned. Anna said, "*Get your butt back to the dining room. Now.*"

The dinner plates were being removed in readiness for the final sanctioned binge of the evening: dessert. George was playing with his DS, and Katie looked bored out of her brain in the absence of food. I think she was pleased to see me. She asked, "What have you been *doing* all this time?"

Thanks to my red carpet chest, I was feeling rather sophisticated. I replied, "... Just powdering my nose."

Katie said, "What? You're a coke-head as well as a stick-insect? Is that how you got so thin? Do you think the white powder would help me lose weight?"

I was gob-smacked. I said, "Listen here, you. Powdering my nose is what glamorous women used to say in the olden days. It's just a polite way of saying, 'I've been taking a piss.' All right? I don't do drugs and neither should you."

Katie said, "Who are you? My *mother*?"

George released a cry of anguish as if he'd just been stabbed. He tossed the DS onto the table and screamed, "The game cheats!"

Dessert was served. A selection of cakes and pastries were wheeled around our table by a dead ringer for Willy Wonka. The sight of all that sugar-rich sweetness sent my head into a spin and, the more eager Katie became, the greener I could feel myself turning. I thought, 'God! I can't believe I used to love cheesecake. What was I thinking?'

Anna praised me. She said, *"You've seen the light."*

Willy Wonka came closer. Ever insightful, Katie said, "I expect you're already full up. So … would you get me a piece of that cheesecake? It looks yummy."

I thought, 'God, help me' and pointed out the cheesecake to Willy. The cake was placed in front of me and we eyeballed one other. Katie suddenly mumbled something through a mouth full of chocolate gateau. It sounded like, "You're being watched."

I said, "What did you say?"

Katie cleared her throat and, without looking up, she said, "2 o'clock. You're defo being watched."

I checked my watch.

Katie said, "No, Dummy! Over there, *at* two o'clock." I looked ahead and slightly to my right. It was the woman from the rest room.

I mumbled, "Who the hell is she?"

It was George who glanced over his DS and said, "You *really* don't wanna know who that is."

Katie said, "He's right for once." Then she smiled and said, "That's Sylvia Mayweather."

I said, "Who? I've never heard of her."

Katie said, "She's a psychiatrist. She goes on TV sometimes and talks about *you know what*."

Her brother looked at me and tapped his nose.

I said, "What? Nose jobs?"

Katie said, "No … *eating* disorders."

I said, "What the hell has that got to do with me? I'm just getting over a bug!"

My wing-men remained silent. And their silence was deafening. The trap-door creaked beneath me.

Anna said, *"Whatever you do, stay calm, or you'll give the game away."*

I thought, 'How did I ever think that people wouldn't suspect!?'

Anna said, *"Screw them. You've finally found something that you're good at. You're looking so much better – like a cat-walk model."*

I thought, 'That woman has probably been spying on me all evening. What if she knows who I am and shares her concerns with mum and dad!?'

Anna said, *"She can't prove a thing. You've just gotten over a nasty virus."*

I asked Katie, "What's she doing here?"

George said, "Hunting down thin people and collecting their scalps. So you've got nothing to worry about, sis."

Katie rolled her eyes. She said, "She's the groom's sister's Aunt's cousin or something. No … wait a minute she's …"

I interrupted and said, "I get the picture." I grabbed my cardi and pulled it back on. The band started playing Pretty Woman and, as my world spun, so did the majority of the guests onto the dance floor.

I found myself alone at the table.

Then I wasn't alone. A woman in a black, strapless dress had plonked herself in Katie's seat. It felt like a visitation from the Grim Reaper. The Grim Reaper spoke. "It's Hally, isn't it?" She sounded friendly but no nonsense. Like a highway patrol woman in a good mood.

I smiled toothlessly. "That's me! Hally by name, Hally by nature."

Anna said, *"Whatever you do, DO NOT babble like an idiot."*

The woman said, "I'm Sylvia. I hope you don't mind my coming over? You've probably been wondering why I've been looking at you."

I picked up my glass and drank some mineral water.

Anna said, *"What's the deal with this bitch? You're a grown woman. Just tell her where to get off."* The trap-door creaked. I took another sip of water.

I said, "You've been *looking* at me. Why? Am I so interesting?"

She said, "I know this is highly irregular, what with this being a function … but, the fact is, I'm concerned about you, Hally."

Anna said, *"Just who in the hell does she think she is? You should bust this bitch's nose. That will shut her up."*

I unclenched my fists. Swallowed hard.

Sylvia said, "You've lost a great deal of weight recently, haven't you?"

I said, "… Bug, thing … my stomach, you know how it is."

She cupped my hand with her own. "I'm a doctor, Hally …"

My head hurt. I said, "You're Dr. *Hally*?"

She suggested I take another sip of water. Then she said, "No. I'm Dr. Mayweather. My particular field of expertise is eating disorders." She removed a card from her black sequined purse and laid it on the table. "I know this must be very awkward … but if you need to talk to someone …"

I said, 'You really have got it all wrong. Honestly! I'm far too sensible to starve myself. I'm not some dysfunctional *teenager*."

She said, "Any time, Hally."

Chapter 9

There was an odd atmosphere in the car as Dad drove us home. Sarah was out for the count beside me. They'd sat her at a table with younger children, I guessed they'd worn her out. Mum and dad had barely uttered a word since we'd set off 10 minutes earlier. I tried to think positive – it was nothing to do with me or that damn woman. They were probably just knackered out after a really exhausting day. Anna said, *"Try to look on the bright side. Maybe they've had a row? That would actually be good. It would take the heat off."*

I thought, 'I don't want that.' The not-knowing was doing my head in and I considered pointing out the fact that they were so quiet. I opened my mouth to do just that but Anna said, *"Are you nuts tempting fate like that!? Even if that quack has spoken to them, they've probably taken her comments with a large pinch of salt. They know you've been ill. They'll have forgotten all about her and her crazy accusations in a couple of days."*

I thought, 'And what if they're so quiet *because* they're thinking back over the last couple of months? It wouldn't take Sherlock Holmes to put two and two together and come up with: Our mad bitch of a daughter has been starving herself.'

Anna said, *"You do trust me, don't you?"*

My mind went blank. Then I thought, 'My family is going to hate me when they find out what I've been doing to myself. They'll probably blame themselves.' I suddenly felt guilty. I needed to talk to someone who understood.

Anna agreed, she said, *"Send Tammy an email as soon as you get home."*

Mum and dad wished me a forlorn, "Goodnight." I went upstairs to my room and closed the door. I felt utterly drained and pulled a bottle of lemonade from under my bed. I poured some into a glass and added maple syrup and pepper. I sat on the edge of my bed and sipped it.

I switched on my computer and wrote the following email: Hi Tammy, are you there? I really need to talk. Can you meet me in the chat room? I sipped and waited. Several minutes passed and I was about to give up when my computer alerted me to a message. I downed the last of the lemonade and opened it. The message read: Sure thing! Give me 2 minutes.

In the chat-room:

Tammy wrote: Hey girl! What's up?

I wrote: I think my stomach bug cover is blown.

Tammy wrote: What happened?

I wrote: A wedding. One of the guests was only an expert on eating disorders! Can you believe that?

Tammy wrote: What kinda 'expert'?

I wrote: The kind of smug know-it-all who writes books on the subject.

Tammy wrote: HOLY CRAP.

I wrote: I was doing so well! It was a 4 course meal and I'd managed not to eat a morsel. I thought nobody suspected a thing. What an idiot! Then this woman gives me her business card and tells me it's okay to call her anytime.

Tammy wrote: Oh my God! Did she talk to your parents?

I wrote: I don't know. But I'm scared. What the hell am I going to do if they confront me?

Tammy wrote: You'll just have to join the club ...

I wrote: No offense but I don't think I'm cut out for the club.

Tammy wrote: Maybe it doesn't seem like it now – but you'll get used to people talking to you like you're nuts. Honest!

I wrote: Are we nuts???

Tammy wrote: They keep telling me I got a disease. But I dunno – what do you think? You're quite the brain box!

I wrote: Brain box? You don't know how funny that is. Disease? Isn't a disease something you *catch*? Anna says it's just a better way of life.

Tammy wrote: I get that. A better way of life. A better way of death. What's the difference, right?

I wrote: Are you serious??? There's a gaping chasm of a difference between life and death! Is that what Anna has been telling you?

Tammy wrote: It's just the way I've been thinking.

I wrote: I have so much to look forward to.

Tammy wrote: Anything's got to be better than being fat. Right?
I wrote: Being dead is better than being fat???
Tammy wrote: We all gotta die sometime.

Chapter 10

"We've all got to die sometime." These had been Tammy's parting words. I climbed into bed and closed my eyes. I could see the words written on the insides of my eyelids – jagged and dripping with blood, they made me shudder. I opened my eyes and the words vanished. I felt so sad for Tammy. Could she really be resigned to the idea of *dying?* At 15? I curled into a foetal position around my pillow and closed my eyes. I wanted sleep, not death.

I was woken by the sound of knocking on my bedroom door. It opened and mum poked her head in. "Can you come downstairs please, Hally."

Her tone was eerily polite. I rubbed my eyes and said, "What time is it? Is everything all right?"

Mum said, "It's almost lunch time. Now please, Hally."

I sat up and reached for my watch on my bedside table. I thought, '12.25! It *can't* be.'

Anna said, "*The shit's about to hit the fan.*"

My mind was all over the place. I thought, 'Is this a dream? Maybe mum's made everyone Sunday lunch?'

Anna said, "*What part of the shit's about to hit the fan don't you understand? Don't worry. I'm not going anywhere. We'll deal with them together. We're a team now.*"

I went downstairs and walked confidently into the living room. After all, they couldn't prove a thing. And if they were going to tell me off for catching a bug … well, let's just say I was determined to have none of it.

Three conspirators were huddled on the edge of the sofa. Their faces expressionless, their body language authoritative. Mum, dad and, horror of horrors, Dr. Mayweather.

Anna said, "*She doesn't waste much time, does she? You should have boffed her while you had the chance.*"

My insides seemed to rush up and settle at the back of my throat. All I could think was, 'I've been summoned to my own execution in a dressing gown and slippers.'

Mum said, "Come and sit down, Hally."

I sat down in the single armchair opposite them.

Sarah came into the room. I'd never been so pleased to see my little sister. Mum said, "Not now, darling. Go to your room."

Sarah looked frightened. She asked, "What's going on?"

Mum said, "We need to talk to Hally. It's nothing for you to worry about."

Sarah turned and looked at me. Her expression said, 'It will be all right ... *won't* it?' She might easily have gloated. I felt proud of her. I wished I was 9 again, too.

Dad said, "Is there something you want to tell us, Hally?" I'd never heard him sound so sad and bewildered. The two women either side of him shuffled nervously. My eyes welled-up. Warm tears rolled down my cheeks.

Mum came and sat beside me on the arm of the chair. She hugged me and said, "Oh, Hally! Whatever the problem is, we're going to fix it. Okay?"

I sobbed, "W ... what problem? There is no *problem*. I'm ab ... absolutely fine. Okay?"

"You don't look fine," said Mum. I gazed up at her. Tears were rolling down her cheeks, too. Mum's the strongest woman I've ever known. I'd never seen her cry. Well, those tears of mum's ... they *completely* melted my resolve. I felt swept away by a tidal wave of genuine love and sympathy.

A blackened penny dropped. I thought, 'It's my family who has my best interests at heart! Not Anna!'

Anna loomed from the darkness. She said, "*Listen to me. If you do something stupid I promise you, it won't* feel *like they have your best interests at heart for long.*"

I thought, 'They're my family!'

Dr Mayweather leaned forward on the sofa and clasped her hands together. She said, "It's good to cry, Hally. Let it all out. You're not alone any more. We're going to help you."

Anna said, "*She means they're going to help fatten you up again. And you know what that's going to feel like.*" The 'life-jacket' that was my body seemed to inflate some, like Anna had *blown* into it.

I shuddered fitfully and sobbed, "It's too late ... you ... you don't know ... you don't know what this feels like!"

Dad said, "What on earth's been going on? I know you caught that flu virus …"

Dr Mayweather interrupted, "That virus cleared up *weeks* ago. It's just been an excuse since then, hasn't it Hally?"

Anna said, *"Typical shrink. Any second now she's gonna pull out a pad and start making notes about us."* She added, *"Don't do it, Hally. I'm warning you. Do not talk to these people."*

I thought, 'These *people* are my family. And they already know. They know! It's too late to go back.' Before Anna could reply I said, "I'm so sorry, Dad."

Dad stood up. He crossed his arms and gazed down at me like I was some pathetic road kill. "Sorry about what, Hally?"

I shrugged and sobbed some more.

Dr Mayweather said, "Hally has been deceiving those that care about her for some time. It's a common symptom of the disease. Particularly in the early stages."

Dad said, *"Disease?"*

Dr Mayweather said, "If my suspicions are confirmed, Hally has anorexia nervosa. It's generally referred to as a disease."

Dad said, "Did she catch it? Could it have been prevented?" His helplessness and ignorance of the situation was making him angry. He said, "And what are the symptoms of this *disease*, apart from the fact that my beautiful daughter appears to be withering away?"

Mum blew her nose. She said, "Sit down, Harry. You're not helping."

Dad sat down, heavily.

Mum looked at Dr Mayweather. She said, "So what's the next step? Where do we go from here?"

Dr Mayweather said, "I'll make an appointment with one of my colleagues at Chelsea and Westminster Hospital." She looked at me and continued, "There's no need to look so desperate, Hally. It's just an assessment."

Mum hugged me again.

Dad said, "Then what?"

Dr Mayweather said, "One step at a time." She stood up and her body language screamed, 'Mission accomplished!'

Mum said, "Thanks for everything, Sylvia."

Dr Mayweather assured her that everything would be all right, that the treatment of eating disorders had come on 'leaps and bounds' in recent years.

Chapter 11

Mum showed Dr Mayweather to the front door. Dad and I sat in silence, listening to the hushed words of the two women saying their goodbyes.

Mum came back into the room and sat beside me on the arm of the chair. She hugged me and said, "I'm so proud of you for owning up, darling. Sylvia said it's the first step … she sounded very positive."

Then, unbelievably, she said, "You must be hungry. I'm going to make your favourite for lunch. Just the way you like it."

Anna said, *"Embrace the sympathy now. Stupid girl."*

I felt the trap-door creak. I thought, 'I'm screwed.'

Dad let out a sigh of relief. He said, "Mum's right. We'll all feel much better after a good meal. You've done the right thing, Hally. Now you've told us, we can help you to see sense again. He walked over, squeezed my hand and kissed me on my cheek.

Mum came back in holding Sarah's hand. Sarah said, "I knew something was weird with Hally." Then she looked at me and said, "I was right. You were hiding something."

I found my voice and said, "You'll make a great private detective some day."

Mum said, "Sarah, go and give your big sister a hug."

Sarah threw her arms around my neck and held on like a little spider-monkey. She released her grip and asked everyone present, "So …what *is* anrexa?" We all gazed at the tiny detective in disbelief. She said, "I was listening on the stairs. I didn't *mean* to. I was just waiting to come back down."

Mum said, "It just means Hally has been off her food lately. That's all. Nothing for you to worry about."

Sarah said, "And that's why she's so skinny?"

Mum said, "Yes. But I'm making her favourite for lunch."

Sarah said, "Roast beef and Yorkshire pudding!" She clapped and spun round like a wind-up toy.

Dad laughed and said, "That's right, Munchkin!" Then, unbelievably, dad said, "It's time we fattened Hally up a bit! What do you think?" He picked Sarah up and placed her on his shoulders like a trophy.

Mum asked me, "What vegetables would you like, darling?" She clocked the look on my face and said, "I'll prepare a selection. You can just pick and choose in a way that makes you feel comfortable."

Anna said, "*Stupid girl.*"

I knew what they expected of me was impossible. I said, "… I'm going upstairs … to lie down for a bit."

"Lunch is ready!" That's what Dad shouted from the bottom of the stairs. He might just as well have said, "Your firing squad is tired of waiting!"

Downstairs, my family were seated at the kitchen table, awaiting the guest of honour. I sat in front of my empty plate and tried not to look at the food. Anna said, "*Look at the food. I said* look *at it. It's steaming. Just like cow dung. In a few moments, they'll expect you to eat it. And boy are they going to be disappointed when you can't. Stupid girl.*"

Dad began to carve the beef. He carved three slices. The anticipation was obviously getting to him. He *had* to see me eat something. "This slice looks delicious. Look, Hally, it's just the way you like it." The following occurred in slow motion: dad plunging a fork into his 'delicious' slice of beef, lifting it, leaning across the table, and releasing it onto my plate. What happened next is a total blank. All I know is, the next time I looked down at my plate, I saw three slices of beef and a mound of steaming carrots and green beans. All swimming in gravy. Someone, I don't know who, said, "Tuck in one and all!"

The trap-door opened ...

The next thing I know, I'm lying on the couch, the side of my head is throbbing and Sarah is bawling at the top of her lungs. Mum screamed, "Just go upstairs to your room, Sarah! Hally's okay. She fainted. She's sleeping. She's fine!"

Dad said, "She's awake!"

Mum said, "Thank, God. Hally, it's mummy. You fainted. Everything's all right."

I tried to sit up but the throbbing in my head increased and forced me down again.

Dad said, "She might have a concussion. I'm going to call an ambulance."

Mum said, "No. You stay with her. I'll call them."

I muttered something about not needing an ambulance.

Dad said, "It's best to be sure. You had a nasty fall …hit your head on the side of the table."

Mum returned with a glass of water. She lifted my head and placed its cold rim against my lips. She looked relieved that I was prepared to take a sip.

I said, "I don't mind water, Mum."

She muttered, "Thank God for that."

Dad said, "It's not surprising you passed out. When was the last time you had a square meal?"

I said, "It's been a while."

Dad said, "How long are we talking here? Days, weeks …?"

I didn't have the energy to lie. I said, "Longer, Dad. It's been longer."

Dad said, "For Christ's sake, Hally!"

Mum said, "Not now, Harry."

Dad asked me if this was the first time I'd fainted.

I nodded.

He said, "Well, at least that's something. If you could have held out a minute longer, you might have got some sustenance into you. A mouthful of beef might have prevented it."

Mum put the glass to my lips again. She said, "Was it the food that caused it, Hally? Was it the food that made you faint?"

I nodded up at her and took another sip. Tears welled in my eyes. I said, "I'm so sorry. I couldn't eat it. I just couldn't. The idea of eating Sunday lunch … you might as well have asked me to drink bleach."

Dad said, "Is the idea of eating really *that* abhorrent? Why Hally? You're not fat! You've always been as skinny as a rake!"

Mum said, "Harry! This is not the right time!"

Dad said, "When is the right time? I'm just trying to understand!"

I said, "I may look skinny, Dad. But I feel so fat. I feel bloated all the time. I'm so sorry."

Two ambulance men came strolling into the room. They looked relaxed, like they were about to hand in a docket and retrieve some dry cleaning.

The first guy had cropped black hair and stubble. He said, "I gather this is our patient?"

He bent down and, having pulled on a pair of rubber gloves, he examined my bruised temple. He said, "Just relax. I'm going to ask you a few questions. What's your name?"

"Hally."

"How old are you, Hally?"

"17."

"What year are we in?"

I told him the year.

"When's your birthday, Hally?"

"August 19th".

Finally he asked, "How many fingers am I holding up?"

I said, "One finger. Ta very much."

Finally, he said, "She's had a nasty bump but there's nothing to indicate that she's suffering from concussion. I suggest she lies down … and gets some rest. If you have any concerns, call your GP in the morning."

Chapter 12

I woke up a couple of hours later. Mum was standing at the end of my bed, her arms folded. She smiled and said, "How's your bump?"

I said, "What's our kitchen table made of anyway?"

"Granite, darling. You caught its edge."

I said, "It's lucky my fat head didn't break it."

Mum smiled. She said, "I've spoken to Sylvia. We're taking you to see a colleague of hers, a psychiatrist, on Tuesday."

"... That was quick work."

"It's just an assessment. We need to know what our options are. Whatever it is you're going through, we're going to get to the bottom of it together, as a family." She left the room and I felt a fleeting optimism.

Anna said, *"This psychiatrist won't be of any use. He won't even know about me. And if you tell him, they'll lock you up and throw away the key. Stupid girl. Everyone you meet from now on will have just one goal – to fatten you up. If that was the answer, you could fatten yourself up. Just put food in your mouth and chew. It's not exactly rocket science, is it? But you can't. Why can't you?"*

I thought, 'Because it's too painful.'

Anna said, *"Because it's unbearable."*

The following morning, Mum came into the room with the phone pressed to her ear. She said, "It's just Sophie. I thought it best to fill her in. You need all the support you can get right now."

Mum handed me the phone and left the room.

Soph came straight to the point. She said, "Is it true? Have you really lost a shed load of weight?"

"It's true."

"Oh my God! You're the last person … why haven't you talked to me? We used to tell each other everything."

"I know. My head's been in a weird place."

"I'm coming over!" She hung up.

Mum must have been listening outside the door. She came back in and said, "I hope I did the right thing calling Sophie?"

I sat up in bed. "She's coming over."

Mum said, "Is that a good thing?"

"I suppose so."

An hour later, Sophie opened my bedroom door.

She tried to hide it but my appearance really freaked her out. She wiped a tear from her cheek. "It was me, wasn't it? This is my fault."

I assured her it wasn't.

She said, "I saw that look on your face when I made that comment about modelling."

I said, "To be honest … it didn't help. Normally, I'd have shrugged off something so ridiculous."

"I know!" Then, in what may have been a first, Soph adopted a totally serious expression. She said, "Everything IS going to be sorted, isn't it? We ARE going to get the old Hally back? Your mum's on the case, right?"

I said, "Mum's been great but …"

"But, nothing!" She felt my shoulders and said, "Damn, Hally! You're skin and bone! You must eat!"

I shook my head.

"Are you crazy?"

"Could be. I've got an appointment with a shrink tomorrow … maybe he can answer that." I was desperate to change the subject. Anything but my possible insanity would do. I asked, "How's Edward?"

Soph shrugged. She has always been a big fan of all things related to that boy. Her silence piqued my curiosity. "No, really. Is Edward okay?"

"… It's not what you think. Charlotte *threw* herself at him. She reckoned he needed 'consoling' or something."

"And?"

"And nothing. All he ever talks about is you."

"He must be madder than I am."

There was an uncomfortable silence.

I said, "… You know, despite all the craziness, I still ..."

"I know you do. Why don't you just *call* him? Once he finds out what's going on, nothing's going to stop him coming to see you."

"It's probably for the best that he doesn't know."

"No way, Hal! You need all the help you can get dealing with this thing."

Anna said, "*You do realise that by 'dealing with this thing' Sophie means stuffing your face just like she does? Three times every single day.*"

I shuddered so hard I actually shook the bed.

Soph threw her arms around me. "Oh, Hally!"

I left Soph on my bed, went into the bathroom and stepped on the scales. The display read: 6 stone 7lbs. I'd lost 2lbs since the previous day. I breathed a sigh of relief. Then I gazed in the mirror and thought, 'What's there to be relieved about! Stop being such an idiot!' I started to well up and muttered, "You really *are* losing the plot."

Anna said, "*Anything's possible. But whatever happens, you're going to stick to the plan. It's not like you have a choice.*"

I thought, 'But why? Why don't I have a choice!? I don't want to put my family through this! They're my family. I love them. I'd *die* for them.'

Anna said, "*Let's hope it doesn't come to that.*" Something inside me snapped. I collapsed to my knees and wailed like a bereaved banshee. A moment later, I heard myself, slapped a hand over my mouth, and watched the door. It flew open. Soph took one look at me and called out for mum. Then she welled up, and backed out of the bathroom.

Chapter 13

At 10.30pm, a strange thing happened. My mobile, which had been buried in my sock drawer for the last two months, began to vibrate. It had somehow escaped the sock drawer and found its way under my pillow. I sat up, reached under my pillow, and answered it. It was Soph. She said, "Sorry! Twice!"

I said, "*Huh*?"

Soph said, "Sorry for freaking out earlier and sorry for plugging your phone in … and leaving it under your pillow."

I squinted at my sock drawer and shook my head. "No problem."

Soph said, "I owe you one more sorry, so, *sorry*, okay?"

"What have you done now?"

I heard some fumbling with the phone and then Edward said, "I miss you."

I sat up and swept my hair out of my face. My heart rate went through the roof. I waited.

Edward said, "Please don't hang up, Hally."

I said, "… Hi."

It was only one syllable, but it must have sounded friendly because he said, "Thank God."

I blurted out, "How are you?"

"That depends on you."

"What?"

I guess he thought I hadn't heard him the first time. So he raised his voice a little, "That depends on you, Hally. I've missed you."

"*What*?"

Edward said, "I've *missed* you."

"Why?"

Edward laughed playfully and said, "How the hell should I know? It's a genuine mystery. Look, can I come over? We need to talk."

I said, "*Talk*?"

"Sophie's tried to explain what's going on. It sounds like you're going through something serious. I should be there for you."

I said, "No way. It's 1am. Mum would go ape if you came over now."

He said, "...Drain pipe job?" In the first few weeks of our relationship, he'd scaled the side of my house several times in his enthusiasm to climb into my bed. Images of him doing the same filled my mind. I suddenly felt horribly fat, like the 'inflate cord' on the life-jacket that was my body had been tugged. I grimaced and pulled my duvet up to my neck.

I said, "There's no way you're coming over."

Edward said, "I just want to talk. I promise. I looked up some stuff on the internet ... I hope you don't mind ... about anorexia."

I felt exposed and violated.

Anna loomed from the shadows. *"Hang up now!"*

I threw down the phone, it bounced off my bed and landed on the carpet. Tears streamed down my face. Anna said, *"You're going to have the puffiest eyes in the history of mankind at this rate."*

Tap! Tap! Tap!

I sat up, startled, and blinked towards the door.

Tap! Tap! Tap! My head swung the other way towards the window. Tap! Tap! Tap! The taps were getting louder. I thought, 'It's him! He's going to wake the whole house!' I climbed out of bed and went over to the window.

Anna said, *"How dare he come over! Push him off the ledge."*

I thought, 'No way!'

Anna said, *"He'll land in the bushes. He'll be fine."*

I released the catch on the window. A body tumbled inside and landed with a thud on the carpet. The body had the nerve to put a finger to its lips and say, "Hush!"

I whispered, "Holy crap, Edward! You have to leave!"

He stood up and attempted to put his arms around me. I said, "No!"

Edward whispered, "I'm sorry. I won't try and touch you. I promise."

His eyes were quickly adjusting to the light. I hurried back into bed. I pulled the duvet up under my nose and peered over its top. Edward was staring at me like I'd lost the plot. He said, "Hally? Can I come and sit ... on the edge of the bed?" I gazed at his athletic outline against the window. It occurred to me that Edward was some kind of hero, come to rescue me.

I thought, 'If only my nemesis were a dragon. Or an axe wielding psychopath.' I felt my hero could have handled one of *those* beasties for sure. Unfortunately, this dragon was *inside my head*. I muttered, "My big fat head."

Edward said, "Your big fat *what*?" He took a step towards me. I didn't react. He took another and then another. He sat down on the bed.

I turned onto my side, away from him.

Edward said, "I had to come. What's going on, Hally?"

I sounded more curt than I'd intended. "I wish I knew. You've seen me now. Please go."

Edward said, "You're going to talk to me. Then I'll go. So … you think you're fat?"

I tutted. "No. I'm not an idiot, Edward. I don't *think* I'm fat. I *feel* fat."

Edward's always been hyper inquisitive. He likes to understand and, unusually for a male, actually listens to what you're saying sometimes. That's one of the reasons I fell for him. So I wasn't in the least bit surprised when he asked, "What's the difference between looking fat and feeling fat?"

I chose my words carefully so as not to disappoint his inquiring mind. I said, "Well, do you ever feel like hitting someone?"

Edward said, "Yeah, of course. Who doesn't?"

I said, "Normally, at those moments, you know you're not actually *going* to hit that person though, don't you?"

Edward said, "Yes. I'm not a psycho."

"Well, like you *know* you're not going to hit that person, I *know* I'm not fat. And like you *feel* like hitting that person, I *feel* fat."

Edward said, "I get that. But how did I get to be the homicidal maniac in all this? What's going on inside that head of yours?" He reached over the top of (what felt like) my mountain of an ass and stroked my hair. It felt nice. I felt like purring. But under the circumstances, I didn't think it would help my case. I also wanted to turn over and face him. But I felt too heavy, like an enormous tree that had been felled. Edward tapped my temple with a finger. He said, "What's going on in there?"

I had nothing to lose now. I said, "There's *something* in there, Edward."

"Something other than your *brain*, you mean?" He shuffled nervously. "Oh God, Hally. Is it a tumour?"

I remained silent and composed my thoughts for, quite frankly, a cruel amount of time. Eventually, I said, "The good news is I don't have a brain tumour. At least, I don't think I do."

Edward breathed a sigh of relief.

I said, "What I've got is *worse*."

"Worse than a brain tumour?"

"Yes. At least there's hope with a brain tumour. A brain tumour can be operated on. Removed. No amount of surgery can remove what's in my head."

"What the hell is it?"

"… It's a voice."

"You're hearing voices?"

This was the first interesting conversation I'd had in months and I somehow found the will to turn onto my back. I gazed up at him. "No. I'm not hearing voices. I'm not a complete loon. The voice is in my thoughts. Exactly like when you have thoughts about stuff." I sat up and said, "Remember how you got thrown out of that exam last year for checking the football scores on your mobile?"

"Like I'm ever going to forget that."

"At the time, you said you knew it was a totally stupid thing to do … but you felt like you *had* to do it. You said you couldn't concentrate because *something* kept bugging you. And that *something* wouldn't let up … not until you'd checked the scores."

Edward nodded. "I felt like I wouldn't be able to concentrate on the exam till I checked 'em. And the rest is history."

"Okay. And remember that *other* time when you kept humming that song? … The one you really hate? And I kept telling you to stop … and then 5 seconds later you'd start humming it again? You said you couldn't get it out of your head. Even though you wanted to because you *hated* it."

Edward shrugged. "It happens to everyone. It's like we can hear songs in our thoughts sometimes, playing on a loop."

"That's right … you could *hear* the song but you *couldn't* shut it off."

"That's true. So?"

"So, I hear Anna in *exactly* the same way as you heard that song. And I can't shut her off either."

"That makes perfect sense. Why are you crying?"

"Because … you're *listening* to me. And maybe I don't sound utterly mental."

Edward brushed some hair from my eyes. "You don't sound mental. Not at all." Then he said, "I totally get it … something in my head that day when I took the exam wouldn't let up … it kept bugging me to check the score. I get that. I really do. But what does *Anna* want from you?"

"She doesn't want me to get fat and … and I think she wants to control me, Edward."

Edward shook his head. "You've always been underweight if anything. And since when did you particularly care about your weight?"

"It's weird, I know."

"Well, why don't you just tell her where to get off? Just tell her no?"

"Like the way you stuck to your guns and didn't check those football scores?"

"That's different. My life wasn't threatened by checking some football scores."

"Look … Maybe I would just tell her no, if I *could*."

"Why can't you?"

My voiced dropped to barely a whisper. "Because she can punish me, Edward, … make me more scared than I thought it possible to be."

Edward brushed the side of my face with his fingertips. He said, "Be gone, Anna Rexia."

"If only it were that simple."

" … I want to kiss you."

Anna loomed from the shadows, "*At last. The true reason for his visit. He's determined to get in your pants.*"

I said, "Anna has just accused you of only wanting one thing from me."

Edward said, "She's right. I do only want one thing. I want the old Hally back." He stood up and walked over to the window. He turned and said, "At least this proves one thing."

"What's that?"

"This Anna bitch … she doesn't know everything."

Chapter 14

The following morning, mum drove me to the hospital for my assessment. Chelsea and Westminster is a modern hospital. You walk through the entrance into a large open space that could almost pass for a shopping mall. Unfortunately, the smell, a mixture of bleach and bandages, quickly dispels any notion of finding that perfect pair of hot pants. Then come the worn-out nurses, lanky doctors in white coats and hordes of wounded, shuffling old folks.

Strangely enough, I felt calm about the assessment. Now that my secret was out, it was as though a burden had been lifted from my shoulders. I felt lighter. Anna was quick to trample on this positive feeling by reminding me how foolish I was being. She said, "*You still feel fat. You still lose the plot around food. Nothing's going to change that.*" I was standing in the lift with mum at the time and the doors had just closed. Mum looked at me and smiled.

Anna said, "*Never forget that this place represents a threat. We're talking interrogations, accusations, feeding tubes, high-calorie shakes and last, but my no means least: WEIGHT GAIN HELL.*" And then she added tunefully, "*These are a few of your least favourite things.*" I felt dizzy and leaned against the side of the lift.

Mum said, "Are you alright?"

I shrugged my shoulders.

Mum said, "It's just an assessment. He's only going to talk to you."

Dr Splicer. The name alone sent chills down my spine. He was younger than I'd imagined; about 40. With close set eyes, round glasses, and a bald patch. He spoke in a bored monotone voice, like he was assessing the safety regulations in a factory. It occurred to me he'd been brainwashed to talk this way by some cult: 'The Cult of The Overly-Educated Professional.' Anyway, without the slightest hint of irony, he said, "Hello. I'm Dr Splicer. I'll be handling your assessment." I couldn't help but smile. He ignored my grin and offered me a limp hand to shake.

Mum said, "Would you like me to wait outside?"

Splicer looked at me. "Do you mind if your mother stays?"

I tried to sound like I had it together. "Of *course* mum can stay."

Splicer smiled toothlessly. He said, "Would you like to stand on the scales please." I felt like I'd been asked to walk the plank. Splicer waved me forward like he was helping me to park. He jotted down my weight.

Mum asked, "Is she terribly under weight, doctor?"

He approached a chart on the wall. "You're 5 feet 9" inches tall ..."

I nodded.

Splicer traced a finger to the answer. "Her BMI is chronically low."

Mum's question was more direct this time. "How much does she weigh?"

"6 stone 2 lbs."

Mum said, "What? She *can't* be under 7 stone."

Splicer said, "The scales are very accurate."

He sat down at his desk and glanced down at my report. "I believe you've spoken to Dr Mayweather?"

Mum said, "That's right. She's a friend of the family."

Splicer looked at me. "It seems she has some concerns about you, Hally."

"I guess so, yes."

"Why do you think that is?"

Anna said, "*Surely, she's written her* concerns *in her report? What the hell is he asking you for?*"

I said, "We were at a wedding ... she saw me behaving a bit weirdly around food."

"And were you?"

"Well. I didn't eat any of it, if that's what you're asking?"

"No. That wouldn't have been overtly strange. It would be perfectly normal for someone, say, if they weren't feeling well or didn't like the food for some reason."

Mum said, "Hally did have a flu virus recently."

I said, "Not all that recently. Remember? The whole flu virus thing was something that ... that Anna wanted me to use."

Anna said, "*I can't* believe *you just said that!*"

I thought, 'It's fine. I want them to understand. They want to help.'

Anna said, "*Idiot girl. They can't help you. They can only punish you.*"

Splicer cleared his throat. Oh so casually, he said, "Anna?"

I said, "Yes, Anna. The voice I hear in my head."

Splicer perked up, like someone had just flicked his interest switch. He picked up a pen and began to write. Anna said, "*Oh, now you've really gone and done it. Mentioning your imaginary friend? Big mistake.*"

I thought, 'Why? The man's a professional. He knows I've got Anna Rexia.'

Anna said, "*Look at him. He doesn't know Jack shit. He's just going to think you're schizoid.*"

Splicer scribbled to the bottom of the page. I thought, 'I'll just explain to him what I meant. Edward seemed to grasp where I was coming from. So Mr. PhD here should find it real easy.'

Anna said, "*Edward's mind is fresh to the subject. This guy's read so many books, he's sat through so many lectures, been told precisely what to think and how to react to the information he receives that, as I'm sure you're about to discover, he is unable to think or function outside his box. Newsflash: I'M NOT INSIDE HIS BOX. But, schizophrenia, on the other hand ...*"

Splicer stopped scribbling. He sat back in his chair and rested his pen on his lower lip. He said, "How long have you been hearing voices, Hally?"

Anna said, "*Told you.*"

I chuckled nervously and looked at mum. It was as though her face had been set in cement. Her expression said, "Just shoot me when you're ready. Would you?"

I said, "Okay, let's just back up here. I never said I'd been hearing voices."

Splicer glanced down at his notes and quoted from them. "'The whole stomach bug thing was something that Anna devised. Anna, the voice I *hear* in my head.'"

I said, "Look. We all have voices in our heads, right?"

Splicer tried not to shake *his* head ... but failed.

I said, "Look, guys. I'm not literally hearing voices." I looked at Splicer. "For instance, there is a voice in your head right now that's telling you I've lost the plot. Right?"

"There's no such thing."

I said, "Okay. I'll rephrase that. There's a voice in your head that's telling you I might be suffering from schizophrenia."

Splicer said, "That's not a voice, that's just me."

Mum buried *her* head in her hands.

I said, "Come on, guys! We all have voices in our heads!"

Mum said, "No, Hally. We don't."

The doctor began scribbling again.

I said, "Well, what about the voice that reminds us to take our keys before we leave the house? Or … or the one that reminds us about our problems the moment we open our eyes in the morning? They're just thoughts, okay? I'm not actually *hearing* voices. Maybe I'm just more attuned to these inner voices than most people or something."

Splicer scribbled for another minute or so. Then he stopped and said, "Let's put the voices aside for a moment."

I said, "You mean the thoughts?"

"Okay. The thoughts. Tell me, Hally, are you obsessed with your calorie intake?"

"Do I count my calories? I know it's common with Anna Rexia to count calories but I haven't been particularly concerned with counting them, no."

"That's interesting. Firstly, you say that counting calories is common with anorexia. Do you believe you have anorexia?"

I looked at mum. And then at Splicer. "I thought that was why I was here?"

Splicer said, "No. You're here to assess whether or not you have an eating disorder. It is by no means categorical at this stage."

I said, "I haven't been able to eat a 'normal' meal in almost 3 months. I think it's pretty categorical. Don't you?"

He scribbled something on his pad and underlined it. *Twice.* He said, "Why do you think you haven't been overly concerned with counting calories?"

I said, "Because I've just been avoiding food that isn't on the 'list.' It's simpler that way."

He adopted an eerily casual tone, "The list?"

"Yes, it's like a short menu."

Splicer tapped his pen on the desk and studied his notes. He said, "Did Anna help you devise this list?"

I was getting frustrated with all the fluffing about. I said, "Yes! Who else?"

Mum said, "Oh, Hally!"

Chapter 15

The assessment could have gone better. After my tour-de-force of giving the wrong end of the stick, I was taken into another room where a male nurse ran some tests on my body. The upshot of these tests saw me admitted to hospital. I was taken to a private room and placed on a saline drip. The next thing I remember, mum is in the room and muttering about having spoken to the medical insurance people and saying that it had all been squared with them.

Earlier, when Splicer informed me of my impromptu stay, I hadn't taken the news *particularly* well. I'll rephrase that. Anna took the news very badly indeed. It was like she assumed control of me for several minutes and had a good old rant at anyone who thought my being admitted was a good idea. I called the hospital staff the following: 'Incompetent! Insane! Berserk! Bastards! Nutters! Barking! Wrong! Delusional! History!'

Eventually, I was handed 3 little pills.

Splicer said, "These will calm your nerves."

Despite Anna's protestations, I downed them in one. They'd left me feeling a bit woozy. Anna was rather worse for wear herself. She began slurring her words. *"We ARE fat. Well? We are. Aren't we? Just because we're fat it doesn't mean we don't have rights. And feelings. Drip?* Drip*!!!? What's in it? Slap the bitch if she tries to stick that thing in your arm! Grab her throat*!"

I swallowed hard, and allowed the nurse to sink the needle in my arm. I gazed up at a transparent bag dangling above me, slurred my words as though drunk. "What's in it? Is it lemonade? I'm only allowed lemonade."

The nurse said, "... It's just a solution. It's going to replace your body's basic nutrients."

Anna slurred, *"It's full of SUGAR. Rip it out your arm."*

I grimaced and thought, 'No way. I'll bleed. I'm not that brave.' I felt the trap-door creak. But thanks to the pills, the trap-door felt so far away, I didn't give a damn. Then I passed out.

When I woke it was dark out. Rain beat against the window. I glanced at a chair in the corner of the room. A black nurse was reading a magazine. I asked, "What time is it?"

She grabbed at the watch face dangling from her breast pocket. "It's 1.30."

I said, "a.m?"

She nodded. "How are you feeling?"

I said, "Weird. Kinda woozy."

She stood up and fiddled with the saline drip above me. "It's all right, Hally. You're in the Chelsea and Westminster Hospital."

I thought, 'I'd gathered that much.'

I felt Anna's presence, like a rat scurrying in a darkened corner of my mind. "*This is it. This is what Tammy was talking about. From now on, everyone's going to talk to you like you're an idiot who's lost the plot.*"

I thought, 'I wonder whose fault *that* is.'

Anna said, "*I'm on your side. I'm the only one who is, remember? Is this bitch going to sit in that chair all night?*" The nurse held my wrist and felt for my pulse. I said, "Have you got to stay with me all night?"

She said, "That's right."

I said, "Seems a bit excessive. I don't need a baby sitter. I'll be okay."

She said, "I don't make the rules, honey. Sorry."

Anna said, "*They think you might try and kill yourself.*"

I mumbled, "*Really?*" Then I said, "I'm not depressed, you know? I get anxious, I'll admit that but not depressed."

The nurse scribbled on the board hanging on the end of my bed. "I know. But I have to stay."

I turned over onto my side and hugged my pillow.

When I awoke the following morning, the nurse was gone and, in her place, mum was writing something in her diary. She glanced at me and said, "Good morning, sleepy. How do you feel?" She stood up and came over.

I said, "Not so bad considering."

Mum gestured to the near empty bag of saline. She said, "I expect it's done you the world of good, darling."

I said, "I am so sorry, Mum."

She stroked my hair. "What for?"

"For becoming a freak of a daughter."

"Stop that. I won't have you putting yourself down."

"If I were a dog, I probably *would* be put down."

"You're not a dog. You're my beautiful, intelligent daughter and you're going to be fine." She bent down and kissed my forehead. I heard the clattering of a trolley outside the room. The door opened and a nurse carried in a tray. She swung a half-moon shaped table over my chest and plonked the tray down on it. Mum said, "Sandwiches … cheese and cucumber. I asked for something that would be easy for you to get down."

"I … I don't think I'll be able to …"

"It's just a *sandwich*, darling. You're going to have to meet the doctors half way. You do know that, don't you?"

I said, "I know that but, even if I wanted to eat it I … I don't think I *could*."

Mum said, "And who's going to stop you?"

Anna made her presence known. "*I am.*"

I said, "Mum, you saw what happened at Sunday lunch. It's kinda difficult to eat when you're unconscious."

"Your body was starved of nutrients then. You would probably have fainted what*ever* you'd been doing." Mum pointed to the now empty bag of saline. She said, "All that goodness will give you the strength you need. I'm sure of it, darling."

Mum's use of the word 'darling' was starting to sound less like 'darling' and more like 'trying', as in 'trying' her patience.

Anna said, "*Go ahead, darling. Show her.*"

I thought, 'What are you saying? That I should *eat* the sandwich?'

Anna said, "*Don't be ridiculous. I'm saying you should show her what happens when you* try *and eat the sandwich.*"

Mum said, "You've turned very pale. It's a sandwich, darling. It won't bite."

I swallowed hard.

Anna said, "*Mum needs to know the score. Otherwise, she'll be standing over you three times a day asking you to do the impossible. It's unfair on her and it's unfair on you. Now, take a bite of that sandwich. Let's set her straight. Let's set them* all *straight.*"

My hand was shaking as I picked up the sandwich, tugged at the cellophane wrapper.

Mum said, "Good girl. You can do it. It's just a sandwich." The wrapping slid away and the smell of cheese climbed my nostrils like a noxious gas. I suddenly felt as though I was on a roundabout that had been *spun* by the playground bully. I must have turned green or something because mum said, "It's okay. It won't *bite*." I sunk my teeth into the sandwich. Mum said, "It's cheddar. You like cheddar. When you were little, it was your favourite."

I gripped the side of my bed and attempted to swallow. As the mulch slopped down my throat, the playground bully *spun* the roundabout faster. I lay down … felt a heavy weight upon my chest. Like someone had stepped on top of me. I bolted upright, gasping, *desperate* to get air into my lungs; desperate to get my 'attacker' off me. My heart thundered to BURSTING point, as though it wanted to squeeze my chest out of my mouth. Mum said, "Hally! What's the matter!?"

I panted, "I – can't – breathe." Mum pressed the emergency call button and ran to the door. I looked at my hands. My fingers had curled them into *tight* fists. I tried to uncurl my fingers … but *couldn't*. My fingers were like strips of curled iron. I thought, 'I'm having a heart attack!'

Two nurses rushed into the room. They took one look at me and their expressions changed from concerned to bored in the blink of an eye. One left the room immediately. The other one said, "You're having a panic attack, Hally. Just take deep breaths and it will pass. You'll feel much better in a minute or two. What brought this on?"

I stabbed a fist at the gnarled sandwich.

The nurse said, "You couldn't get it down, then?"

Mum shook her head, turned her back on me, and gazed out of the window.

The nurse said, "Would you like to try something else?"

I looked at Mum's back, wondered if she was crying.

I said, "No … not right now."

Anna said, "*Looks like Mum's finally got the message.*"

Chapter 16

Dr Mayweather was outside in the hall, talking to mum in hushed tones. They came in and stood either side of my bed. Dr Mayweather said, "How do you think your assessment with Dr Splicer went, Hally?"

Anna had been right. I was beginning to feel more like a victim than a patient. The initial wave of support and understanding had washed right over me. And left me feeling exposed and vulnerable. I said, "You're the expert. Why don't you tell me?"

Mum said, "Hally! Sylvia is here because I asked her. Seeing your reaction to taking a bite out of that sandwich earlier ..."

Dr Mayweather said, "It's okay, Angela. Hally's head is all over the place at the moment."

I said, "... The meeting with Splicer could have gone better. I somehow gave him the impression that I'm hearing voices ... that I'm schizophrenic."

Mum nodded her head and blew her nose into a hanky. Dr Mayweather said, "And what do you think about that, Hally?"

I said, "I have never heard voices. I was just talking about my thoughts, that's all. I can't help it if the guy gets all excited at the prospect of unearthing a genuine nutter."

Dr Mayweather reached across the bed and squeezed Mum's arm. She said, "I really don't think that Hally is a candidate for schizophrenia at this stage. From what you've described of Hally's reaction to that sandwich, it's probably best if we concentrate on that for the time being."

Mum said, "She had a *panic attack*. How can anyone have a panic attack because of a mouthful of bread and cheese?" Mum and I both awaited Dr Mayweather's reply with bated breath.

She flicked a dark curl from her face. "Hally may have developed a phobic reaction to food."

Mum said, "Is that common with eating disorders?"

Dr Mayweather said, "Clearly, a common symptom of anorexia is a negative reaction to the idea of eating. The degree of this reaction fluctuates from patient to patient." Then Dr Mayweather looked down at me and asked, "Have you had a nervous reaction of this severity around food before, Hally?"

I said, "Apart from passing out at the dinner table at home? No. Why would I? Those are the only two times I've been forced to eat something that wasn't on my list."

Dr Mayweather said, "Dr. Splicer mentioned you had a list. What's on your list, Hally?"

I said, "The Lemonade Diet, watercress soup and Ryvita."

Mum said, "What is the Lemonade Diet?"

Dr Mayweather said, "It's a high-energy, low-calorie drink."

Mum said, "What's going to happen if she can't get any proper food down her?"

Dr Mayweather said, "In the short term, we may have to look at providing Hally with a nutritional supplement direct to her stomach."

Anna said, *"The bitch is talking about force feeding you. They're going to stick a tube down your throat and inflate you like a balloon. Pleased with yourself now?"*

Dr Mayweather looked at me. "It's okay. It's not as bad as it sounds – it's a little uncomfortable."

I said, *"Really?* A little uncomfortable? You're going to stick a bloody great tube down my throat."

Anna said, *"Look on the bright side. Maybe you'll choke to death. Problem solved."*

Dr Mayweather said, "The tube's actually not that big." She made a tiny space between her thumb and index finger. "They'll provide a sedative. I've been told the pills Dr Splicer gave you yesterday were effective in reducing your anxiety?"

I said, "They really did help."

Mum said, "What about the long term? She can't spend the rest of her life being fed with a tube ... spaced-out on God-knows-what."

Dr Mayweather said, "There are a number of options. One-to-one counselling is usually a good place to start. I know you got off on the wrong foot with Dr Splicer yesterday but he's a leader in his field."

Anna chuckled. *"He's the leader? Of what? An army of psychiatrist lemmings?"*

Mum said, "You seem to have a better rapport with Hally than he does."

Dr Mayweather said, "At this stage, Dr. Splicer is better suited to the task of helping Hally to re-evaluate her relationship with food and her own body. I'll be keeping a close eye on her progress."

They left me alone.

Anna whispered, "*Make a run for it. Your clothes and shoes must be in that closet.*"

I thought, 'I'm in enough trouble. I'll end up in a padded cell if I try and escape. They only want to help me. Who knows? Maybe they can?'

Anna said, "*How can they help you? They're utterly clueless about me. Look, you can't even cope with a bite of sandwich. What's gonna happen when they shove a tube down your throat and pump weight-gain bile into your stomach?*"

I thought, 'They're going to give me some more of those pills. You must admit, they did help yesterday. I didn't care about anything, not even the trap-door opening.' The trap-door creaked. A nurse came in holding a little cup. It contained my pills. I downed them in one.

A few minutes later, Sophie came into the room holding a bunch of grapes. She clocked my reaction and said, "Sorry! I wasn't thinking. I'll eat them." Then she threw her arms around my neck and hugged me.

I said, "I've just taken some happy pills. If I start making even less sense than usual, you'll know why."

Soph said, "Oh, Babe! What are they *doing* to you?"

"They're about to force feed me, kiddo."

"You are joking?"

A male nurse wheeled a contraption into the room. He hung a bag from a hook at its top. The bag was transparent and contained a thick orange-brown liquid. Soph put a grape in her mouth and started to chew.

Anna said, "*Maybe she'd prefer popcorn and a soft drink?*"

Soph said, "That stuff must be really good for you."

The nurse shoved one end of a tube down into the 'meal.' He left the other end dangling and left the room. Soph couldn't help herself. She squished a grape between her teeth and said, "…So, where are they going to stick the other end of the tube? They're not going to …"

I said, "No, they're not!" I pointed to my throat.

Soph said, "Oh! Okay." Then she said, "Edward told me about his visit. Pretty romantic."

I said, "It was a hell of a shock at first. But, the boy came good in the end. Did he say anything to you?"

"He told me to tell you that he's 'on the case.' He's determined to help you."

I said, "The boy's heart is definitely in the right place."

Soph mumbled, "And so is the rest of him."

I told her off for looking. The pills were really starting to take effect. I said, "I'm feeling pretty good now. If you know what I mean." I winked at her.

Soph said, "The pills?"

I said, "I must find out what they're called."

We both giggled. A male nurse came back with mum in tow. He began fiddling with the contraption he'd wheeled in earlier.

Soph said, "Do you want me to wait outside?"

Mum answered her. "I expect it would be for the best."

I shrugged my shoulders. Soph squeezed my hand and left the room.

Chapter 17

That night, the chair in the corner of the room was empty. No idea why. Staff shortages perhaps? Or maybe Splicer was pleased with his progress. If he was, I was happy for him. The tube-feeding that day had been hellish. Even with the happy pills, it felt as though they were coaxing a snake down my throat – a snake that had been trained to regurgitate its kill into my stomach.

At midnight, a nurse came into my room. She checked my blood pressure and jotted her findings down on the clipboard at the end of my bed.

She left the room and Anna said, *"It's all about damage limitation now. We have to do something about all that crap they've pumped into you."*

I thought, 'Maybe it's doing me some good?'

Anna said nothing. Instead, I felt my body 'inflate' in the usual, terrifying way. I sat up in bed, held my stomach, and groaned. Anna spoke now. *"Go into the bathroom and look in the mirror. We need to see how much damage they've done."*

I clambered out of bed and flinched as my feet touched the cold floor. The mirror in the bathroom was small. I had to stand on tiptoes just to see my chest. I started to feel repulsive, like my body was a sack filled with sewage. I prodded my tummy and felt my fingers being consumed by rolls of fat. I looked down. I couldn't see the fat but I could feel it all right. I groaned in agony and quickly placed a hand over my mouth. Anna said, *"Vomit."*

She didn't need to say it twice. I pulled up the lid of the toilet as though if I were suffocating and my only source of oxygen was within. It smacked against the wall. Anna said, *"Quiet! If they catch you they'll tube feed you!"* After I'd hurled, I felt better. So Anna suggested I do it again. And *again.* Until all I brought up was air. I lay on the floor and gazed up at my toothbrush and toothpaste by the sink. My breath stank. It took a serious effort just to stand and clean my teeth, let alone follow Anna's next 'suggestion'. She said, *"Now we need to burn off some of that blubber."*

I gazed in the mirror and murmured, "You got a lighter or something?"

Anna said, *"It's nice you haven't lost your sense of humour. Now Jog. On the spot."*

I said, "I don't think I *can*." I felt my body ballooning again, even after all that vomiting.

"Okay! Okay, I'll jog …" I lasted about 30 seconds before I collapsed to my knees, and sobbed quietly into my hands.

The next morning, I had a visit from Splicer. He bounced into my room carrying a chair which he placed next to my bed. He said, "Good morning! How was your night?"

I mumbled, "A laugh-a-minute, thanks."

He retrieved his notes from a briefcase and sat down, cradling them to his chest. He said, "I've been thinking about our talk yesterday and I'm very interested in hearing more about these thoughts of yours, the ones you've given a name to."

I was in no mood to play games. "Dr Mayweather doesn't think I'm hearing voices."

Splicer cleared his throat. "It's important to explore all relevant possibilities."

I said, "Presumably that would include the *relevant possibility* that I'm not actually hearing voices?"

He ignored my remark, opened the file and retrieved a pen from inside his jacket. "Right!" he said, "Is there anything you want to ask me?"

I shook my head. After all, what was the point? The guy was so in the dark about Anna that he might as well have been a pair of cartoon eyes, blinking in the dark. He blinked and said, "I'd like you tell me more about Anna."

"What do you want to know?"

"When did you first realise that Anna was something outside, *separate* from you?"

It sounded like he was still barking up the schizophrenia tree. I gave him a stinging look.

He said, "I have an open mind. So, if you can cast your mind back …"

I looked away, wondered if I could trust him. This guy had the power to section me. Lock me up and throw away the key. He said, "Go on, Hally. I'm here to help …"

Anna had fascinated me from the start. I hadn't realised *how much* until the night Edward came to my room, and asked questions about her. I suppose it didn't take very much to encourage me to drop my defences on the subject. I gazed down at my hands. "I remember the exact moment Anna pitched up. A friend of mine made a comment. She said that I was too fat to be a model. And then a few weeks later … when I was at a low point ..."

"Yes?"

"The comment … it came back to haunt me. And so did Anna."

He leaned forwards. "And what does Anna sound like?"

I glanced sideways at him. "Well, I'm not hearing voices so … she sounds a lot like me … like she's trying to impersonate me. I suppose that's how she gets away it."

"Gets away with what?"

"… Fooling us, her victims … making us believe that *her* views are *our* views."

He said, "That's interesting ..." and began scribbling on his pad. "So … Anna's been with you ever since she reminded you of that comment: 'You're too fat to be a model?'"

I nodded, "Since then it's like she's become my boss. And I think she can …"

"Yes?"

"... punish me."

His eyes widened. "And how does she punish you?"

I shut up and studied him. He looked like a kid who had managed to get his hand in the cookie jar but couldn't quite reach the *nuttiest* cookie. I decided to give the jar a shake for him. I said, "She can make me anxious. And she's clever."

"Clever? How is she clever?"

I said, "Sneaky clever. She knows every trick in the book."

"By tricks, you mean ways to avoid eating?"

I said, "That … and much more besides."

He stunned me by asking a halfway intelligent question. "If you could see Anna, what would she look like? An angel or a devil?"

Anna said, "*Tell him I look like an angel. A guardian angel.*"

I said, "That's actually a good question. She might say that she looks like my guardian angel."

Splicer cleared his throat. "Did Anna just tell you to say that?"

I remained silent. I'd be damned if I was going to give this guy *more* than enough rope to hang me with. I said, "I've answered your questions. Is there any chance you might answer one of mine?"

He took off his glasses and sat back in his chair. "What would you like to know?"

I leaned closer to him. "What do *you* think Anna is?"

He put his glasses back on. "I really couldn't say. That's for you to tell me, Hally."

I rolled my eyes. "I'm tired now. I need to take a break."

Chapter 18

"It's for you to tell me, Hally." This had been Splicer's reply when I'd asked him what he thought Anna was. He's supposed to be the expert. Not me. What the hell was in all those text books he read anyway? Anna said, *"They instructed him in the art of wearing down the nutter by asking wave upon wave of probing questions. They told him to collect enough babbling data to write a book and make a ton of dough. I told you the guy wouldn't have a clue about me."*

I thought, 'Someone must know what's going on inside my head.' The door opened and Edward crept in. He closed it quietly behind him and grinned like an idiot. I looked at my watch. It was 12.28am. I was really pleased to see him. So I said, "What the hell are you doing here? It's gone midnight!"

He whispered, "Keep your voice down. I had to sneak past the nurse's station."

"And everyone thinks *I'm* nuts?"

"I had to come."

"You pick your moments. Be warned, they check on me every 30 minutes." I glanced at my watch again. "... and they're due any second."

"Get rid of her!" He darted into the bathroom and pushed the door to.

I whispered, "Brilliant, Edward ! I'll just strangle her with my drip cord and stuff her body in the closet. I'm sure Splicer will be *thrilled* with the new twist for his book."

I heard the nurse approaching. I turned onto my side, pretended to be asleep. I thought, 'If that boy sneezes, we'll both be in deep shit.'

I felt her checking the saline drip in my arm … and then she left the room, closing the door behind her. I sat up. Edward poked his head out of the toilet. "Has she gone?" I nodded. Edward came over and sat beside me. He said, "You're pleased to see me. I know you are." I was finding it increasingly difficult to look pissed off. My frown turned into a smile and … he *kissed* my cheek.

I said, "Steady on!" I sounded like an old fossil from the 1950s.

Edward said, "Talking like someone's gran? Is that a side-effect of anorexia?"

"No. But extreme physical violence is. So watch it."

Edward glanced at the contraptions on either side of my bed. "They've really been putting you through it, haven't they?"

"I can't lie ... the room service in this hotel leaves a lot to be desired."

He poked my right temple and said. "Have they made any progress sorting out what's going on inside this gorgeous head?"

"My shrink thinks maybe I've gone all schizoid. He's in two minds about it."

"Which would make him schizoid, right?"

We giggled. It relieved some of the tension. Edward said, "You told him about Anna? Like you told me?"

"Yes. But he wasn't nearly as understanding."

Edward stood up. He clasped his hands behind his head and looked up at the ceiling.

I said, "You got something on your mind?"

"I don't know if I should mention this now." He sat down beside me. "I don't know if it's even important."

I was obviously curious. "Just tell me ... I'll let you know if it's important."

"I've heard about this guy ... an *old* guy ... used to be a professor of science ... at a university up north. I think he ...that he might be able to help you."

"*Really*? What? Did he become some all-powerful wizard in his retirement?" That sounded more sarcastic than I'd intended it to.

Edward said, "You wanted to know."

"Sorry. I could really use an all-powerful wizard about now."

"I'm serious. Tony's been seeing the guy for extra maths tuition."

"I don't think algebra is going to be much use with this one."

"Tony really likes the guy. Says he's got all these insights ... into how our minds work ...where our thoughts come from ... stuff like that. From the way Tony was talking, I think he might be able to help you to understand what Anna's about."

"Well, that's a bit of a long-shot, don't you think?"

He shrugged. "That's why I wasn't sure whether to tell you. I mean, I wasn't going to say anything but …"

The nurse came in. She said, "I thought I could hear voices. How did you get in here? It's way past visiting hours."

Edward held out his wrists as if to say, 'Handcuff me if you like.'

Then he said, "Bye, Babe. You will think about what I said?"

I nodded and smiled.

My hero was escorted from the room. I reasoned that his name would be mud in this fine medical establishment from now on. I lay down and thought, 'What was that all about? He *thinks* some old maths teacher can help? Full marks to the boy for trying, though.'

Anna was quick to agree. She said, "*He has nice buns but there isn't a lot going on upstairs, is there?*"

I thought, 'Shut. Up. He's a clever guy. Intuitive. Insightful. Christ, he actually listens! You must admit, he took on board what I told him about you a lot better than Splicer.'

There was no reply.

I suddenly felt a flicker of hope, like a tiny window of opportunity had opened. Through this pin-prick of a window, I imagined a wise old man – a sage who could answer *all* my questions. I did my best to ignore the negative thoughts that Anna was now pitching at me on auto-pilot. I fell asleep grasping this new life-line and hoped it would still be within reach in the morning …

Chapter 19

The next morning I woke up and gazed about my room. It took me several seconds to register where I was. How diabolical things were. I sank back down onto my pillow and thought, 'Didn't something *positive* happen last night? A tiny window of hope? Oh, yeah! Edward's found me a wizard!'

Anna said, "You really are losing the plot."

I impressed myself by telling Anna to shut up, again.

She was quiet for about half a minute. Then she said, "Let's go and look in the mirror."

I thought, 'God. Do I have to?'

The trap-door creaked, and my heart began to pound. 'Okay! I'll go and look in the mirror!'

I elevated myself on tiptoes and gazed at my reflection. The agony I'd felt the previous day returned; my body once again felt like it was swelling and ballooning out of control. I collapsed onto my knees at the base of the toilet and was about to stick my fingers down my throat when a nurse poked her head around the door. She said, "What are you doing, Hally?"

"I … I feel sick."

"Okay … it's very common for patients being fed by tube to have an upset stomach. Come out of there and I can give you something for that."

"Okay. But I need to go to the toilet. Would you mind closing the door?"

"I'll close it a little … but I'm going to stand right here and wait for you."

Anna said, "That bitch isn't going anywhere. You'll have to abort. If she catches you hurling, they'll tube feed you again right away." The ballooning sensation lessened.

I got up and barged past the nurse. She said, "Dr Splicer will be in shortly." Then she grabbed the waste paper basket and used it to wedge open the door to my room before she left me 'alone'.

Anna said, "The bitch is going to tell Splicer about her suspicions."

I climbed into bed. 'Quite honestly, I'm past caring.'

Splicer bounced into my room. Incredibly, he announced that we were "making progress." Anna suggested he was talking about his forthcoming book deal. One thing we could all agree on was what Splicer described as "The way forward." This would see me discharged the following day; returning to the hospital three times a week for what he described as "counselling sessions, check-ups and nutritional assistance." I didn't care. I just wanted out of there.

Chapter 20

The next day at noon, Mum came to take me home. They'd force fed me again at 7am. The anti-anxiety meds were wearing off by the time Mum arrived. I felt more gross than ever. We were halfway across the parking lot when Anna said, *"You need to vomit up some of that crap. I mean right now. Tell mother you need to rush back in and use the loo … or else you're going to pee your pants."*

I thought, 'She'll never buy it.'

"Then don't give her an option. Just sprint back."

I kept walking towards the car, resolute … and then the trap-door began to creak and shudder beneath my feet. I stopped dead, as though Anna had tugged my reins. "I'll be back in a tick, Mum! I really need a pee."

Mum looked startled. "Really?"

"Really. I'll be two ticks. Promise." The look on her face tied my stomach in knots. But I couldn't risk falling through the trap-door. Not in public. So I sprinted across the parking lot and back into the hospital. I had to stop and rest against a wall. I held my side where I had a terrible stitch. My breath was racing. I thought, 'I feel about a hundred years old!'

Anna said, *"You'll feel better once you've got some of that stuff out your fat belly."*

I thought, 'Really? I feel like I'm running on empty already.'

"As soon as we get back you can have some lemonade diet. It's stashed under your bed. Now go!"

In the rest room, I keeled over the cubicle and stuck my fingers down my throat.

That night, I lay awake in bed thinking. I was no nearer finding a solution to understanding Anna. If anything, my sessions with Splicer had left me feeling more isolated. Not only did he not know about Anna but spent most of the time asking me to fill *him* in. I desperately needed to focus on something positive. All I had was this old guy Edward told me about. So I clung to that; like a person who'd lost everything apart from one rusty old coin she was going to use to buy a lottery ticket. This old man's genius, the jackpot that could make everything right. Edward had called a couple of times. I'd found out his name was Ken, and that he was really keen to meet me. But, what if it became clear within the first 10 seconds of our meeting that Ken understood about as much as Splicer? Or even less. I reassured myself that that wasn't really possible. Obviously Anna didn't help. She wanted this little avenue of hope closed a.s.a.p. "*You need to go meet this nutty old witch-doctor as soon as possible.*"

Edward called me at noon. Mum smiled as she handed me the phone but I could tell my appearance was eating her up inside. I hated what I was doing to her. To all my family. Sarah had been bundled off to stay with an aunt, and dad looked tired and gaunt. Thanks to me, he'd visibly aged in a week. It was heart-breaking. I waited until mum had left the room.

"Hi, Edward ."

"Hey. You okay? You sound kinda weak?"

I whispered, "Anna … she's got me throwing up … *all* the time … she's trying to purge me of all that gook they fed into me in hospital."

"Isn't throwing up what *you* want to do?"

"I'm so weak, Edward. I don't know what I want."

"Well … *resist* her."

"Ah … unfortunately it's not that simple. Like I told you, she can punish me … make me feel a thousand times worse." Tears welled in my eyes. My voice dropped to a whisper, "She … she can kill me."

"And how can she do that?"

I wiped away my tears. "Are you kidding? She's killed so many, *thousands* … Edward, what if ..."

"You're not going to die, Hally ..."

The emotion in his voice shook me. I said, "Arrange a meet with this teacher guy. I mean do it *now*. I want to see him … I'm talking *today*. He may be my last hope."

"And what? She'll let you meet him? Anna? Just like that? Won't she try and stop you?"

"She wants me to meet him … she wants me to find out that he's just as clueless as everyone else."

"I'll call him now and call you right back."

I hung up the phone.

Anna said, "*Good. Let's get this farce over and done with.*"

The phone rang, startling me. I answered it. Edward said, "It's all arranged, Hally. Ken will be waiting for you on the fourth floor of Selfridges department store … in the Garden Café at 3pm tomorrow. I've only got a couple of lectures tomorrow. I'll bunk off and come with you."

"I'd rather do this alone."

"I rather you didn't."

"Please, Edward. I don't want any distractions. I'll call you as soon as I get back. Thank you. Thank you for everything."

Chapter 21

The following morning, Mum was fussing round me. She hadn't left the house in three days. Not since she'd brought me home. She was fluffing up my pillows. I said, "If you want to get out … do a food shop or something, then go ahead. It's not like I need a nurse maid 24/7."

"That's okay. Your father's doing the shopping."

"I'm not suicidal, Mum. We could both use the space."

"I'm not leaving you alone today." She picked some clothes up off the floor and left the room.

The phone rang. Mum picked up the extension downstairs in the kitchen. I sat up and listened. Mum was *definitely* in the kitchen, talking to someone. I climbed out of bed and walked unsteadily to my closet. I didn't need Anna's advice about what to wear. Even though I felt like a hippo, I looked like a bag of bones. Anna had countered my observation by whispering, "*Perhaps … but you're the biggest bag of bones anyone has ever seen … and these bones of yours are dripping in fat.*"

I pulled a black sweatshirt/jogging pants combo from the closet and got dressed. I was actually out of breath. So I sat on the edge of my bed, rested my chin on my collar bone, and stared down at my bony knees. I thought, 'I must look utterly pathetic.'

Anna said, "*You do. You* are."

'Ho hum.' I reached under my bed and retrieved a full bottle of lemonade, the energy giving ingredients already added. I drank the bottle dry, burped and stood up. I thought, 'I just hope that's enough fuel to get me into town and back. I'll take the bus both ways. Less walking that way.'

I walked, more slowly than I'd intended, onto the upstairs landing. Mum was still talking on the phone. She was in the kitchen but the kitchen door was open. I'd have to pass it to get to the front door. I returned to my room and went to the window. 'It will just have to be a drain pipe job.' I opened the window, swung my legs out, and felt for the drain pipe. If the neighbours had been watching, they must have thought the starving inmate at number 40 was making a run for it. I guess they weren't wrong.

Chapter 22

Selfridges is a massive department store. You walk through the main entrance to be greeted by women selling perfume and make-up from behind shiny, brass rimmed cabinets. I made a bee-line for the lifts, avoiding eye contact with anyone.

As the lift carried me up towards the fourth floor, I felt a rush of excitement, like I was embarking on an adventure. I had no idea why. Anna tried to burst my bubble of optimism with a well stuck pin. *"Look on the bright side. The old guy might come in useful for a bit of extra maths tuition. He might not even be some old perv."*

The Food Garden Café was larger than I'd imagined. An intimidating space to find someone you've never met. It was noisy, too: the voices of shoppers re-fuelling between bouts of credit card abuse, vs the clatter of cutlery and impatient children. I stood in the middle of the place and scanned the tables for an elderly man sitting alone. All I could think was, 'Where's my wizard hiding?'

I spotted a hand waving at me from behind a potted fern. A face appeared beside the hand and mouthed, "Hally?" It was a pale face capped with a full head of silver hair. He was just as old as I'd imagined, I estimated in his late 70s. I felt very self-conscious as I edged my way past the noisy tables. My wizard stood slowly, and offered me his hand to shake. His grip was firm. He smiled, his face transformed by intersections of lines and dimples. His forehead was massive.

I thought, 'He must have an *enormous* brain inside there. Could it really be big enough to help me, though?'

I glanced down at the table. Big enough to seat six, its surface buried beneath A4 papers and folders. My wizard said, "I'm delighted you could make it. I'm Ken. Do excuse the mess." I must have looked exhausted because he didn't wait for my reply, he just said, "Sit. Please, sit." His accent was familiar yet distant and at first it was difficult to place. Then the penny dropped. I realised he sounded like a commentator from one of those 1940s news-reels. I imagined him saying, "Hitler has invaded Poland. As a consequence, this country is now at war with Germany."

I sat down opposite the aging man whose voice belonged to the past and said, "It's really kind of you to meet me."

"Not at all …" He began collecting up his papers, most of which contained maths equations, and stuffing them inside various folders.

I said, "Is this your office?"

"It is rather. Since I retired from teaching full time, it's become a handy location. I've been coming here for many years. The acoustics are wonderful. All this white-noise helps me to relax, no end."

"It just sounds like a drone to me."

"That's because you haven't learned how to utilise sound." The man was clearly a little eccentric but, so well-meaning with it, I didn't mind one bit.

I was so relieved when he came straight to the point. No faffing about with unhelpful questions. "So, I understand you're being tormented by an annoying, persistent and rotten little voice in your mind."

"Yes. I am. But I'm not actually hearing voices."

Ken adopted a forlorn expression. He said, "My dear girl, has someone suggested that you are?"

"I've seen a psychiatrist at the Chelsea and Westminster Hospital …"

Ken held up a large palm. It might as well have had 'say no more' written on it. He said, "I expect you'd like to know what this voice is?"

"Yes, more than anything but …"

Ken held up that palm again, this time it read 'Don't worry. I'm just about to tell you.' He said, "I can see you're thirsty for answers. Some might even say *parched*. So, what's your first question?" He sat back and smiled. Such a kind face.

I couldn't help smiling with him. I looked into his learned, blue eyes, leaned forward and said, "Like Edward told you, I have this voice in my head. I call her Anna. What is she?"

Ken rubbed his ample belly. "I'm so pleased you've started with an easy question." My mouth fell open. Ken said, "Anna is a *tiny* memory cell … albeit one with a terrible agenda." He stabbed a sheet of paper with a pencil and wrote 'Anna' above it. As I gazed down at the dot, he said, "Anna is a mere pinprick of electricity and neurons. Just one amongst many millions in your mind. Unfortunately, she's emerged as top dog due to all the attention you've been lavishing on her."

I nodded enthusiastically. "That's true. I have been."

"And how could you not? Anna has been so demanding of your time."

I heard myself sigh with relief at this insight. "... So, you think Anna is a memory cell?"

"I *know* she is. I've spent the last 40 years studying her sort. Not only in my own mind … but also in the minds of my students … those with an interest in such things."

"You've had students with eating disorders?"

He shook his head. "We all have our inner demons, of one sort or another. And no matter what name we give to them, Mother Nature has ensured they all adhere to the same set of rules."

"Which are?"

"Firstly, these particular memory cells, which I call Trip-Wire Cells, gather information … information about our particular fears. And then they use this information to remind us about our fears …. and frighten us."

"But *why*?"

"To protect us."

"From what?"

"From that which we've convinced them is a terrible threat."

I went bright red. "… You mean like being too fat to be a model?"

"Is that your particular fear?"

I nodded. "For a time."

Ken said, "Anna would have emerged in your mind at a time when you'd reached a low point emotionally. Her first question to you would have been something along the lines of, 'Is being too fat to be a model REALLY a threat?' And, unfortunately, because of your low emotional state, you would have answered, "Yes!" Ever since that moment, Anna has been doing her best to protect you from this 'threat.'"

I felt tears well in my eyes. "That's *exactly* what happened."

"I didn't mean to upset you."

"I'm sorry. My head's all over the place at the moment. Lack of food. Lack of sleep. Lack of understanding. I'm *lacking*."

Ken stood up. He said, "How amiss of me. What would you like to drink?"

"I don't suppose they have lemonade?"

"Well then you suppose wrong. They have the finest lemonade in London. He winked. I won't bother asking you if you'd like something to eat. I can tell you're not ready." Then he looked into my eyes, correction, he looked *through* my eyes, as though he were talking to something beyond them, and said, "Yet."

Ken returned with my lemonade. I thanked him and drank it down greedily. I plonked down the glass. My mind was so full of questions it actually ached a little. "You said Anna *thinks* she's been protecting me?"

"Yes."

"Well *how*? How has Anna being protecting me?"

"By keeping you away from the one thing that could turn your fears into reality. Food."

Even though I felt I knew the answer to my next question, I needed confirmation. "How does she achieve this? How does she keep me from eating?"

"Oh, it comes so very easily to Trip-Wire Cells like Anna. You see, Mother Nature has provided Anna with some powerful weapons."

I swallowed hard. "And these are?"

"For starters, she can cause intense feelings of anxiety, panic or depression."

I nodded and punched at the air. Then I whispered as though I didn't want Anna to hear. "It's like I have this trap-door, right underneath me *all the time*."

"How extraordinarily perceptive you are."

"I am?"

"Your trap-door analogy. It's quite brilliant."

"Thank you."

"I can help you to understand how this trap-door works with a short story. If you'd like?"

I nodded so hard I practically stabbed myself with my chin. Ken said, "It's about a man who is lost in the desert. The poor man is desperately tired but also desperately thirsty. Therefore, he has two opposing memory cells or 'voices' in his mind. The one responsible for making sure he doesn't die of exhaustion tells him that he 'Must stop and rest!' But the other voice, the one responsible for making sure he doesn't die of thirst, tells him he must 'Keep on walking and find water at all costs!' These two voices will battle away inside his mind and attempt to persuade him to follow *their* instructions. Now, one of these voices has access to an emergency lever and can have the final say whether the man likes it or not. Can you guess which one, Hally?"

I thought for a moment and said, "Is it the sleep voice?"

Ken said, "Precisely! It can pull a lever and cause the man to faint."

I shuddered and folded my arms across my bony chest. This was such an important piece of information, I felt I needed confirmation of my confirmation. "So, Anna *does* have a kind of lever ... one that opens the trap-door?"

"Oh, yes. And she's been using it like a spoilt child in order to get her own way."

I shuddered. "In the beginning, I actually thought she was *helping* me ... to keep the trap-door closed. What an idiot."

"Don't be hard on yourself. That's what Anna wanted you to believe. It's what's made you dependent on her. But the truth is this: every bout of anxiety or panic you've experienced since this ghastly business began, has been as a result of Anna throwing a tantrum and pulling the lever to get her own way." A little girl at a table behind us burst into tears and started screaming and banging a spoon against the table. Ken said, "Just like that."

Chapter 23

Ken told me I'd taken in quite enough for one day. And he suggested that I go home and think about what he'd said. "Give me a bell, Hally … if you decide you want to learn more." I'd memorised the mobile number he'd given me before I'd even put it into my pocket. I was on the train going home and *buzzing* because someone finally understood me. More than this, Ken had been able to answer my questions in a way that made perfect sense. It had always felt like Anna was trying to protect me from something. Until recently, I thought it was from the anxiety. After all, she would tell me what to do and it would stop. But what Ken told me made more sense: the crazy bitch had been trying to protect me from food. And she'd been using the trap-door to make sure I avoided eating.

Anna rushed from the shadows, startling me. "The man's just a senile old nutter. He's conning you."

I thought, 'You would say that.'

Anna said, "Where would you be without me? You'd be obese, that's where."

Tears welled in my eyes. 'If you don't let me eat, I'm going to die of starvation or have a heart attack. Is that really what you want? Talk about cutting off your nose to spite your face!'

Anna said, "Eating and getting fat are THE greatest threats you face."

I thought, 'Oh. Really? Greater than the threat of dying?'

Anna said, "Eating and getting fat are THE greatest threats you face."

I thought, 'I'm putting my family through hell!'

Anna said, "Eating and getting fat are THE greatest threats you face."

I thought, 'You sound like a damn recording! But maybe that's to be expected of a memory cell. Come to think of it, you've been regurgitating the same crap for months!'

Anna said, "It doesn't matter what you think. I'm going to protect you whether you like it or not. That's my job. You'll thank me in the end. You'll be thin and beautiful and in control of your life."

'In control? That's a joke! You're the only one who's in control.'

"I am you."

'No. You're just a tiny part of me. The size of a damn pinprick apparently!'

"I may be small, but I'm all-powerful. And that's because I've been tasked with such an important job. Protecting you from your greatest fear."

"But I don't care about getting fat anymore! I just don't care!"

"I don't believe you."

As I walked home from the station, I resolved not to tell mum and dad about Ken. They could easily jump to the wrong conclusions and stop me meeting him. Anna had obviously been listening to my thoughts. And she did the most underhanded thing she had done so far: she impersonated my voice. And she did it in such a way that I believed I was listening to my own voice, my own thoughts. So, I heard myself think, 'Wait a minute … I must tell mum and dad about Ken. They're on my side. If I vouch for Ken and tell them how much sense he makes, they'll believe me! Besides, there's no way I'm going to faff about and meet Ken in secret. I'm not a child. No … that would just complicate things. I can make my own decisions. The last thing I need right now are more complications. I'm fighting for my life!'

By the time I'd arrived home, Anna had wound me up to the point where I was bursting to tell mum and dad about Ken. I walked into the living room and said, "I have the most amazing news ever!"

Mum threw down the magazine she'd been reading and jumped up. "Where the hell have you been? I've been worried sick!"

I said, "I've been to see someone who understands what I've been going through!"

Mum said, "But your appointment with Dr Splicer isn't until tomorrow."

I said, "Oh God. No. I'm not talking about Splicer. This guy knows what I've been going through. He's super intelligent. A retired teacher. His name is Ken. Mum, he just explained the whole deal to me about Anna!"

Dad folded his newspaper and put it down. He said, "What are you talking about, Hally? Where did you meet this man? At the hospital?"

"No. In Selfridges."

Dad said, "What? The department store?"

I explained how Edward had arranged the meeting. I told them what Ken had said and how it had all made perfect sense. They listened patiently and even nodded from time to time. I thought I'd got through to them. At least, I did, until mum looked at dad and said, "I'll go with Hally to the hospital tomorrow. I'll explain the whole thing to Dr. Splicer. This Ken person can't have done too much damage."

I said, "Mum! What are you talking about? Weren't you listening? I think Ken can really help me."

Mum said, "You're just starting to make progress with Dr Splicer. We can't jeopardise that because of some man you met in Selfridges."

I said, "Progress! What progress? Nothing's changed!"

Mum said, "Nonsense. Dr Splicer is very optimistic about how things are going."

I said, "I'm sure he finds it all very interesting. But I don't! All he does is ask questions. I need answers!"

Dad said, "He needs you to answer his questions before he can answer yours."

I stormed out of the room, slammed my bedroom door, and called Edward on my mobile. He answered before the second ring. "Hey! How did it go?"

I said, "The guy is a wizard. You were right, Edward. I think he can help me."

"Well then, why do you sound so down?"

"Because I made the mistake of over-estimating my parents' intelligence."

"You told them about Ken?"

"I must have been mad! They totally freaked."

"They'll calm down."

"Really? They've placed all their hopes in that idiot interrogator at the hospital."

"Offer to meet them half way … tell them you'll keep talking to this Dr. as long as you can see Ken. It would be like … like a complementary therapy."

I said, "Great. Now you're overestimating my parents' intelligence." Someone knocked on my bedroom door. I said, "I'll call you back."

Mum came in and sat down on the stool in front of my dressing table. She said, "Look, Hally. I've discussed it with your father and we're prepared to do whatever Dr Splicer advises. If he thinks it's a good idea for you to keep talking to this man in Selfridges, then, fair enough."

I said, "Splicer will never go for it. The stuff Ken was talking about was way outside his 'box'."

Mum said, "He's the professional. He's the expert. We must abide by his wishes. Surely you can see that, Hally?"

"It doesn't really matter what I see. Does it?"

Chapter 24

Splicer looked more witless than ever. He was behind his desk twirling a biro round his fingers and reading something in my file. Finally, he looked up at mum and said, "I do share your concerns, Mrs Winters." He switched his gaze to me and said, "I don't think it's a good idea for you to confide in anyone who hasn't been properly trained, Hally."

I looked at Mum and said, "You've already told him about Ken? *When*?"

Mum said, "I gave Dr. Splicer a call first thing this morning."

Splicer said, "I don't know what this man has told you, Hally, but there are no quick fixes here."

"Ken never said there were any!" I looked at mum as if to say 'What the hell have you been telling this guy?' I said, "Look, he just gave me a great insight into what I'm going through. He let *me* ask the questions for a change."

Splicer said, "As I said, I don't think it's a good idea to confide in anyone who hasn't been formally trained."

I said, "Are you *deaf*? I didn't confide. I didn't have to tell *him* much at all. He just knew."

Splicer said, "How on earth can this man make a proper assessment of your situation without a thorough briefing?"

I said, "He has insights ... into the human condition ... how all our minds work. How else can you explain how he knew so precisely what I'd been going through without my explaining it to him?"

Splicer said, "It's a trick, Hally. How much money is he asking for his help?"

I crossed my arms. "He hasn't asked for a penny."

Splicer said, "Hally, it's important that you refrain from meeting this individual during your treatment." He looked at Mum and said, "Once things are in order, it's unlikely she will want to have contact with this man. She'll be thinking clearly again."

I said, "Who is '*she*' exactly?"

Splicer ignored my comment. He cleared his throat and said, "Then there's the question of the boyfriend."

I gasped and said, "What are you on about now?"

Splicer said, "The boy who has been encouraging you to meet this man in Selfridges? I think it would be wise if Hally severed contact with this young man for the time being."

Mum said, "It's so very difficult with teenagers."

Splicer said, "Has Hally increased her calorie intake since she's been home?"

Mum shook her head.

Splicer said, "One step at a time." Then he paused and said, "I've been giving it a great deal of thought and, in light of recent developments, it would be advisable if Hally spent some time in an eating disorder clinic. I can more readily work on her case along with dedicated professionals who will monitor her closely."

I said, "*What*?"

Mum said, "How long would she have to stay?"

Splicer said, "Well, that's up to Hally. It could be as little as just a few weeks."

Mum took hold of my hand and squeezed it tenderly. She said, "Would that be your recommendation, doctor?"

Splicer looked at me. He said, "I know it seems daunting now, Hally. But, given time, I'm sure you'll see the benefits."

Anna said, "*The doc's right about the benefits for once. You'll meet some interesting girls in this place. You'll be able to compare notes. Maybe even learn a thing or two.*"

I muttered "Oh, it sounds just brilliant."

Splicer said, "That's very good, Hally. You're starting to see sense." He smiled at mother. And I groaned.

I was being carried, on a wave of convention and tunnel vision, away from the one person I had any faith in. Splicer picked up his phone and dialled the number of the clinic. I felt like a fish caught in a net. Splicer spoke into the phone, "I have a patient who needs a place as soon as possible." He jotted something down and then hung up the phone. "Good news. They'll have a bed for Hally on Thursday." Thursday was in two days' time. Splicer said he'd like a word with mum in private. He asked me if I wouldn't mind taking a seat in the waiting area just outside the door.

I sat down and stared into space. My mind was a total blank. I felt cold and put my hands inside my jacket pockets. I felt a piece of paper. I pulled it out, stared at Ken's mobile number. I thought, 'It's now or never.' I dialled the number. As it rang, I gazed at Splicer's door, willing it to stay closed.

Ken said, "Hello."

"Hi, Ken. It's Hally."

"I'm so pleased you called."

"You are?"

"Oh, yes. I've been thinking about your problem and have devised a plan of attack for you."

"Really? Will it enable me to get Anna's hands off those levers?"

"Oh, yes. But it will require considerable effort on your part. But if you're up for the fight of your life?"

I said, "*Whatever* it takes. Listen Ken, I have a bit of a problem. I'm at the hospital now and they've booked me into a clinic from this Thursday."

Ken went silent. The door to Splicer's consulting room opened slightly. The conspirators were finishing their conversation just inside the door. I whispered, "Ken?"

Ken said, "Not to worry. I'll devise a crash course. I can equip you with the weapons you need to fight Anna in an afternoon. Clearly, the battles that follow will require rather longer."

"It will *have* to be tomorrow, Ken. But where?"

Chapter 25

My meeting with Ken was to be at St. Luke's Church, on the edge of Regent's Park. Ken had explained that the basement of the church was used by a primary school and that the vicar allowed him to use it for private tuition on Saturdays. "The classroom is a good size. And we shall need all the space if we're to prepare you for battle." To say my curiosity was piqued was something of an understatement.

Since I'd come out of hospital, it had felt like I'd been under house arrest. It was Saturday morning, and I awaited my opportunity to escape nervously. It came at 9.30am when the phone rang. I stuck my head out of my bedroom door and heard mum talking on the phone in the kitchen. I muttered, "Sorry, mum. It's gonna have to be another drainpipe job." Mum had locked my bedroom window and taken the key. But she'd hidden it where she'd been hiding stuff since I was 6, in dad's sock drawer.

Some kids, who were riding past on their bikes, stopped and gawped at the stick-thin prisoner making good her escape. I jumped off at the bottom, my legs folded beneath me, and I rolled over. Then I got up and moved as swiftly as my legs would carry me in the direction of the station. The sound of cruel laughter faded behind me. And, for what felt like the *millionth* time, I told Anna, 'I'm going okay! So SHUT IT!' Oh, and one more thing: I *thanked God* that Anna only seemed able to open the trap-door when food was involved in my disobedience. Otherwise, I'd never have been able to leave my room. Maybe it was just as well that Anna Rexia didn't have a buddy called Agra Phobia.

St. Luke's is a lovely old church. I opened an iron gate and walked into a graveyard. Ken told me to go down a flight of steps at the side of the church. "Locate the blue door," he'd said. And he was very specific about this. If the door was not blue, I was not to continue under any circumstances. Thankfully, the door at the bottom of the old stone steps was indeed blue. He'd told me that the bell was not working and I was to tap on the frosted window. Almost immediately, there was movement within – a blur of grey and brown which grew larger. A bolt slid to one side. And then the door opened.

Ken was dressed in the same clothing as our previous encounter: tweed jacket, white shirt and dark green corduroy trousers. He said, "The vicar's about! He might pop down occasionally."

I said, "Is that a problem?"

Ken said, "No. He's perfectly pleasant. Forewarned is forearmed and all that."

I thanked him for his consideration.

We walked under a number of low, stone archways and into a primary school classroom. Drawings and paintings and photographs of pupils were stuck on the walls. The desks had been moved to one end of the classroom, their chairs up-turned on them. At the other end of the classroom, two chairs stood opposite each other. We sat down on them. Ken produced a whistle and placed it between his lips. For about 30 seconds, we sat and stared at each other in silence. Then he blew his whistle, *right* in my face. It startled me so much that my bottom leaped several inches from the chair. Ken removed the whistle from his lips. "Interesting."

I said, "Are trying to make me a nervous wreck?"

He smiled and complimented me on my insight. Then he reached down and picked an object off the floor. It was one of those wishbone shaped contraptions that weight lifters use to strengthen their grip. He handed it to me. I placed it between my fingers and thumb in the correct way. He said, "Squeeze it together." I attempted to press the two foam covered levers together. They didn't budge. I apologised for being weak and pathetic. Ken took back the hand-grip and placed it on the floor beside his chair. He said, "Have you heard of the fight or flight response?"

I said that I had but that I didn't really know what it was. Ken said, "It's our primitive survival response. Once activated, it releases anxiety causing adrenaline into our blood stream. This adrenaline makes us frightened and jumpy and is supposed to assist us in taking flight from danger. When I blew the whistle just now, you jumped pretty high."

"I'm a regular athlete."

Ken said, "The reason you jumped so high was because of the sudden activation of your fight or flight response and the release of adrenaline. If there had have been real danger, and not just an old chap blowing a whistle in your face, you would have been able to bolt through that door like a gazelle."

I said that I didn't doubt it but I'd rather he didn't do it again unless it was strictly necessary. He told me that he never did anything unless it was strictly necessary. Then he said, "Whenever this trap-door of yours opens it means that your fight or flight response has been activated and anxiety causing adrenaline has been released into your bloodstream. And that's *all* it means. Without exception, every ghastly palpitation, hot flush, beating of butterfly wings in your stomach, wave of dread and sudden pounding of your heart is caused by your fight/flight response. And the same is true for every human being on this little planet."

I said, "So, fight/flight is a bad thing, then?"

"Not if we're being chased by a hungry tiger, then it's actually quite useful. But, if we're contemplating eating a cheese and pickle sandwich? It's a very bad thing indeed."

I nodded and said, "Sometimes I get this weird feeling … it's like my body is being inflated like a balloon. It makes me feel disgusting. What's all that about?"

Ken said, "It's just a version of the fight or flight response. The chemical component is altered slightly to achieve this effect."

"And tell me again what part Anna plays in all this?" I rolled my eyes. "I don't think I can hear it enough times."

"As you so eloquently put it, Anna has her hands on a 'lever' that's causing it. Although, it sounds as if she has 3 or possibly 4 levers: one for general anxiety, one for panic attacks and another for this horrid ballooning effect."

I said, "And she just picks and chooses the lever depending on the situation?"

"That's right. Whichever one she thinks will best protect you from eating or gaining weight."

I said, "What can I do? Can I stop her?"

"Oh, yes. But a great battle lies ahead. And while I can equip you with the weapons you need to win this battle, you must wield them yourself. Are you ready?"

"*Ready*?"

"To take this fight to Anna?"

"Are you *serious*? The way things are going, it's now or never."

"Then I shall equip you with the weapons you need."

Chapter 26

The wizard had promised me weapons. He got up and left the room. I imagined he was visiting his stash of arms and would return carrying a shield, lance and helmet in my size. I was a little deflated when he reappeared carrying a plate of chocolate biscuits.

Ken placed the plate on a table and, without looking at me, he said, "What has caused your sudden attack of nerves, Hally?"

I said, "That would be the biscuits."

"That's not actually true, is it?"

"Isn't it?"

"No. The biscuits have *triggered* your nervous reaction. But what has actually caused it?"

I thought for a moment and replied, "… My fight or flight response?"

Ken said, "That's right." He walked towards me with the plate of biscuits. He sat down and rested the plate on his knees. "You suspect that I'm going to ask you to eat a biscuit. And your little passenger, Anna, is monitoring this potential threat. She has given the lever a little *tug*. This amounts to a gentle reminder that 'biscuits are a no-go area.' Now, if I were to ask you to eat a biscuit, her tug would become greater and, if you actually attempted to eat one, she would show no mercy at all, and PULL the lever with all her might!"

I gripped the sides of my chair with all *my* might. "That about covers it."

Ken said, "I'm not going to ask you to eat a biscuit. What would be the point? We know what would happen. You need weapons to quell your fight/flight response and you don't have them yet." He got up and, once again, I imagined he was off to his weapons locker.

This time he returned with a mug of tea. He sat down and said, "There is only one way to quell the fight/flight response and shore up the trap-door." He nibbled on a biscuit and some crumbs fell onto his jacket. He brushed them off and said, "Any ideas on that score?"

I reaffirmed my grip on the chair. "Can't say I have a single one."

He said, "The best way to quell the fight/flight response is by manufacturing feel-good endorphins."

I had images of a factory with great vats of feel-good endorphins being stirred by men in white overalls.

Ken placed his mug on the floor next to his chair.

He clasped his hands together on his lap, dislodged some biscuit from the inside of his cheek with an odd facial maneuver and said, "We are all capable of manufacturing these glorious, uplifting endorphins using the tools that Mother Nature has provided us."

I was all ears, like an enormous bunny with a minute head and body. I shook this unhelpful image from my mind. Ken said, "We can manufacture them during a particular type of exhale."

I said, "Huh?"

He said, "... Exhale."

I said, "I got that. But I don't get that."

Ken said, "Whenever we humans are involved in an enjoyable, uplifting activity, the emphasis of our breathing is *always* on our exhale. For instance, when we laugh; or cheer; or sing; or whistle; or groan because we're enjoying a good massage, the emphasis is *always* on the exhale. Never the inhale. The only times the emphasis is on the inhale is when we're startled. Like when someone blows a whistle unexpectedly. Or fires a gun. Or gives us dreadful news." I thought about that for a moment. And it made perfect sense. Ken said, "To produce the feel-good endorphins that we need to fight anxiety and panic, it's about the huff, the puff and sometimes even the *roar* ... from here." Ken pointed to his abdomen. He winked ... and that's when he let rip with a deep, sustained roar. During Ken's roar, his lips curled and his eyes narrowed and I considered getting the hell out of there. Then his face lit-up with a satisfied and friendly smile. He chuckled and said, "I really needed that."

" ... I could ah ... I could tell you enjoyed it."

Ken said, "I did enjoy it. It felt like pure relief. And the reason it produced this feeling of well-being? Well, that's because I activated the (feel-good) endorphin pump that Mother Nature, in her infinite wisdom, placed in our abdomen. You see, when the abdomen is compressed by a deep and sustained exhale, like a cheer or a belly laugh, it sends a message to our glands; one that says we are experiencing something *positive* ... and that we fully deserve a release of feel-good endorphins."

"Okay." He asked me to stand up with him. We stood toe to toe. "Now," he said, "it's your turn. I want you to *force* the air from your belly using your abdominal muscles." He prodded me just above my belly button and said, "Imagine butterflies are swarming in your belly ... and you intend to force them UP and OUT of your mouth. Remember, it's vital that you expel your butterflies from *here*." He prodded my abs again. "Ready?"

I took a deep breath and went for it: A MIGHTY ROAR. I somehow managed to sound like a frightened kitten, mewing. *And* I spat in Ken's eye. Ken blinked several times and re-focused his gaze on me.

I said, "Sorry 'bout that."

"Dear girl, that wasn't even *2%* of the effort that's required to quell the fight/flight response."

He picked up the hand-grip and handed it to me. He told me to squeeze it again. I attempted to but, just like the first time, I couldn't budge it.

He said, "Now, on the count of three, I want you to exhale from *deep* within your abdomen and, at the same time to produce a battle cry of 'Come on!' Oh, and squeeze the hand-grip."

"Are you sure? I wouldn't want to frighten the vicar."

"Never mind the vicar. He's a forward thinking fellow and he'd be rooting for you if he were here. No more excuses. They originate from Anna. Are you ready?" I grasped at the hand-grip. Like Anna, it felt immovable, and I wondered how he *ever* expected me to find the strength to overcome its resistance. Ken said, "Ready? One ... *two* ...three!"

I *really* went for it this time, found my exhale and *crushed* the butterflies swarming in my belly. And, at the same time, produced a throaty battle cry of "Come on!" I fell silent ... and enjoyed a feeling of intense relief.

Ken pointed to my hand. "Look!" My knuckles were red and the hand-grip was fully closed within my grasp. Ken said, "This is a true gauge of your inner strength, Hally."

I began to cry.

Chapter 27

Ken instructed me in the art of producing this powerful exhale from deep within my abdomen for another 30 minutes. With each new battle cry of 'Come on!' the hand-grip was crushed. And I was getting a natural high from the feel-good endorphins I was producing. It kinda felt like I'd been cheering a racehorse; one I'd put my *entire* life-savings on and had cheered over the finish line in first place. I had become a little light-headed but, due to the endorphins, I felt stronger and more confident than I had in a long, long time. It was at this point that Ken offered me a biscuit. I was buzzing and, without giving it a second thought, I reached out and took one off the plate. It suddenly struck me that I was holding a biscuit. Not just any biscuit but a chocolate biscuit with a sugary fondant centre. I listened for the creak of the trap-door. Nothing. Ken said, "You're perfectly safe for the next few minutes. Go on. Take a bite."

I took a bite. "Is that *it*? Am I cured?"

"No. That wouldn't have been much of a fight now, would it?"

I said, "What fight?"

Ken said, "Exactly. The fight's to come." He looked at his watch and said, "In fact, round one of this fight is on its way." Then he glanced at the door as if expecting some muscle he'd hired to walk in and boff me.

I nibbled, "So why's Anna so … quiet?"

"She's been silenced by those feel-good endorphins you've been making. Put simply, she can't get at the levers, which means she can't punish you for your actions … *yet*. Think of it this way: it's like Anna is floating in a pool of your positive endorphins. And she'll have to wait until the pool drains … only then can she reach her levers again."

I said, "So, to clarify: the levers are at the *bottom* of the pool and the pool is draining slowly? And as the pool drains, so does this great feeling?"

"As ever, your insight is remarkable."

I held up the hand-grip and furrowed my brow. I said, "Why don't I just keep filling up the pool?"

Ken said, "That's not practical. And besides, Anna can float about in this pool indefinitely, waiting for her chance to reach those levers."

"So what now?"

Ken chuckled like a naughty schoolboy. He said, "Anna is going to be rather livid when she finally gets hold of those levers – she'll be like an angry bull; enraged, she'll charge at you with the intention of punishing you."

I said, "Well, that can't be good."

Ken reached down for another biscuit and took a bite. He nibbled, "It is good. The only way to defeat this bull, Anna, is by leaping onto her back and riding her until she collapses from exhaustion. Like breaking in a wild stallion. Once you've done this, it will signify the winning of round one."

I said, "*Ride* her? How do I ride her?"

"Well, when she charges (starts yanking her trap-door levers) you're going to leap onto her back. By this I mean, launch your counter attack."

I asked him what he meant.

He said, "It's quite simple. Instead of giving up and cowering like you've always done in the past ..."

"I didn't think I had a choice."

"I know. But now you do. So, instead of cowering, you're going to fight back by *swamping* her in endorphins, thereby giving her a bloody nose."

I said, "She'll go *nuts*, Ken."

"Indeed she will. Which is why you must keep your guard high and protect yourself at all times."

"How?"

"By continuing to pump the feel-good endorphins, *no matter* what she says or does."

Chapter 28

Ken walked to the other end of the classroom where he assembled about twenty chairs into a mini arena. He said, "It's not quite the Roman Coliseum but it's the best I can do at such short notice."

I said, "I expect you'd like me to stand in the middle?" Ken pulled back a chair and created an entrance. I walked through it, clutching my hand-grip. Ken replaced the chair. I stood in the centre of the circular space and felt a twinge of trepidation. I said, "The pool is draining. I can feel it. I ate 3 chocolate biscuits. I must have been *mad*. My throat … it's bone-dry."

Ken said, "Anna is close to her levers now. She could pull one … and come charging at you at any time. Now, she might charge at you from *this* direction." Ken motioned to the space beside him. "Therefore, you might experience the rush of an oncoming panic attack." Then he walked several paces around the arena. He stopped and said, "Or, she might charge at you from here. And make you feel like your body is ballooning." He took several more steps and said, "Or, from here! And make you feel more anxious than you've ever felt in your life. From whichever direction she charges at you, Hally, what are you going to do?"

I croaked, "… Ah, run like hell?"

Ken said, "I know you're joking but, in all seriousness, if you run, she will trample you into the dirt. You must stand firm. You must fight her. How are you going to fight her?"

I said, "I'm going to jump onto her back and throttle her."

Ken said, "How?"

I attempted to grasp the hand-grip but my hand was shaking now and I *couldn't* get a firm hold on it. Despite this, I swallowed hard and said, "I'm going to exhale from my abdomen … and pump feel-good endorphins into my body."

Ken said, "That's right. Remember, she's going to attack using a multitude of hellish feelings. And during this attack, you're going to counter-attack by creating feel-good endorphins. It's vital that you KEEP ON pumping these endorphins until she backs down and you no longer feel threatened. Keep on filling the pool with positive endorphins, *just* as you did earlier."

I said, "Oh God, Ken! She's here! She's charging at me!"

Ken said, "From which direction?"

I pointed and said, "Ballooning Ken! I'm ballooning! She wants me to throw up! It's the only way to stop this! It feels like I'm going to burst!"

Ken said, "Fight!"

I collapsed to my knees and vomited the biscuits onto the shiny blue floor. Ken left the room.

He returned with a bucket and mop. I was slumped on one of the chairs, surveying the scene of my mugging through sad eyes. I said, "Ken. I'm so sorry."

Ken began to mop up the mess. He said, "No apology necessary. With the possible exception of the regurgitated biscuits on the vicar's floor, that's the outcome I expected from Anna's first charge."

I stifled my tears and said, "*Really?*" Then I blew my nose.

Ken said, "Oh, yes. It was important that you experienced 'balking' from the outset."

I mumbled, "Balking?"

Ken said, "That's right. If a racehorse approaches a difficult fence, one it doesn't think it can get over, it will come to an abrupt halt; sometimes throwing its rider to the ground. This means the horse has *balked* at the idea of jumping the fence. A few minutes ago, you balked at your first hurdle, and collapsed when you should have been fighting."

I nodded sheepishly.

Ken said, "You balked because of the myriad of doubts that flew into your mind and told you to give up; to throw in the towel because resisting the tidal wave of anxiety was futile."

I said, "That's exactly what happened. How did you know? I'm so pathetic."

Ken sat down and rested his chin on the mop's handle. He said, "You have nothing to berate yourself for, Hally. Those doubts were not your own."

I said, "Anna?"

"Of course. She impersonated your voice, as she has done in the past. She sent a volley of doubts that destroyed your resolve. And she was *so* successful that you collapsed and offered no resistance at all. Not a single drop of feel-good endorphin was produced for your counter attack."

I blew my nose and said, "Anna Rexia … she's such a clever, brutal bitch."

Ken said, "Now it's your turn to be the clever one; and the brave one; and the stubborn one who refuses to back down. This time you'll know what to expect. Remember, she can only *persuade* you to surrender your counter attack by convincing you to balk. She can't *make* you, Hally." Ken left the classroom. He returned with another plate of biscuits. He said, "Let's coax the beast out again, shall we?"

I felt comforted by the fact that I couldn't possibly put up a more pathetic showing this time. I thought, 'Okay, *bitch*. Bring it on,' and bit into a biscuit.

Anna charged.

The room span about me. My heart pounded at my ribs. My breath grew short. And a feeling of utter dread and hopelessness clawed at my insides. Anna *rushed* from the shadows: "*You WILL fail! You ARE hopeless! You cannot resist MY demands! You ARE fat! You ARE ugly! You ARE pathetic! You WILL vomit up that biscuit or you WILL die!*"

I looked at Ken. He held up a hand-grip of his own and said, "Now would be a good time to fight back. On the count of three: one, two, three!" We exhaled and roared together.

Another wave of anxiety crashed down on me, tried to carry me off and dash my resolve against the rocks. But this time I stood firm and screamed, "Come on!" as I throttled the hand-grip and pumped relief-giving endorphins into my body. A minute later, and to my exquisite surprise, the waves of dread and panic had washed over me. And the biscuit was still in my belly.

Ken said, "Stand firm, Hally! Keep your defences at the ready."

I nodded as Anna charged again. My response was the same: squeeze, pump, stomp, scream "COME ON!" and snarl like a crazed banshee fighting for her life.

Ken was now pacing up and down, willing me on. "Keep fighting! Keep pumping the endorphins! Don't back down!" A couple of minutes later, exhausted and surprised, I stopped. The vicar walked in whistling 'All Creatures Great and Small.' He went to a locker and began twisting the dials on a combination lock. He glanced over at me. I must have been a curious sight, encased within a prison of chairs, wild, blond locks falling across my face. I was panting, and felt like a cave woman who'd just wrestled an angry predator out of her cave.

The vicar switched his gaze to Ken. He winked and said, "Exorcism, Ken?"

Ken chuckled. "Anna Rexia."

The vicar said, "She's awfully thin, Ken." Then he sought my gaze from behind my wild locks. "Whatever's troubling you my girl, give it hell."

He removed a bag from the locker and marched out waving his free arm like someone shooing away a persistent fly. Ken said, "Take stock, Hally. Take stock of how you're feeling."

I was panting, my heart was racing but the only discomfort I could feel was the ache in my hand where I throttled the hand-grip. I said, "I feel good. I feel *really* good. Only my hand hurts."

"Excellent! It shows you applied the appropriate effort. And the anxiety?"

"… *What* anxiety?"

Ken patted my back. "You've done it, Hally. You've won your first round against Anna."

"*First*? How many rounds are there?"

"You will need to defeat Anna in a similar fashion, perhaps another ten, twenty, or maybe thirty times … and you'll have removed her hands from those levers."

I said, "Another twenty rounds you think?"

Ken said, "Yes. But not right now. Right now, Anna is regrouping. She's battered and bruised and licking her wounds. It is during the next week or so that she'll make these attempts at reasserting her authority. Take heart; with each defeat she suffers she'll grow progressively weaker and, should you continue to employ this level of effort against her, then, there will come a time when her great charges will feel more like pathetic pokes. Until she pokes at you no more."

Chapter 29

When I left the church, I felt buoyed by an incredible sense of achievement. Then I remembered that I was going to be put in a clinic the following day: a clinic where I'd be watched 24/7. If I tried to mount my offensive against Anna there, I'd be moved to another clinic: one with a padded cell reserved for Hally and Anna. This was a joke. At the exact time I needed space to fight, I was due to have my space invaded by strangers who would quickly reach the conclusion that this panting, snarling woman was a maniac.

I arrived home at 10pm and spied mum and dad through the living room window. Dad was pacing up and down and mum was sitting on the sofa; her arms folded, her gaze drawn to her wristwatch every few seconds. I reasoned that I was in deep shit but that I had no choice but to explain the situation and hope, beyond all reason that they'd listen. Who was I kidding? I put my key in the front door and muttered, "Here goes nothing …"

Mum shouted, "Hally? Is that you?"

Dad came bounding out of the living room. He said, "For God's sake, Hally! What do you think you're playing at?"

Mum skirted around him. Arms still folded, she said, "Where have you been? Tell me you haven't been to see that old man from Selfridges?"

I said, "I have been to see that old man from Selfridges and I know how to fight Anna. I *fought* her, Mum."

Mum said, "For pity's sake, Hally! Anorexia is a disease, not a person!"

Dad put his arm around her. He said, "She'll learn all about it at the clinic."

I said, "About the clinic, I think it might be a good idea to put it on hold for a couple of weeks. Only ... there are some things I need to try first." Their shared expression of horror told me I had their undivided attention. So I pressed on. "Look, I'm sure the clinic is a *fine place* and that they do a great job and mean well and everything but …"

Mum went bright red and began to quiver, like an incendiary tomato. She said, "But *what,* Hally?"

"But ... as good as their approach *probably* is, I expect it's a bit long-winded. If I can just be left alone, I may be able to overcome Anna. And I mean *really* overcome her. Throttle her. For good."

Mum screamed, "You're delusional, Hally! Stop this ridiculous talk, right now!" She quietened down to a near whisper. "Just go to bed. We're leaving for the clinic at 9am. I've already packed your suitcase."

I sat down on my bed, spied the suitcase, and shuddered. My head was muddled and I needed to talk to someone. A faint voice, way in the back of my mind said, *"Why not email, Tammy? Hers is the voice of reason."*

I thought, 'Hers is *not* the voice of reason. She's in the thrall of a monster like you. Just shut up and let me think.' I felt Anna reaching for one of her levers but, mercifully, she didn't have the strength to pull it. The butterflies she'd created fluttered momentarily, and died.

Anna said, *"I'm getting stronger all the time. I'm recovering. And I'm going to teach you a lesson you'll never forget. You think you know what fear is?"*

I muttered, "Take your best shot."

"You have no idea little girl. I will strike when you're in a room full of suspicious, judgemental people. You'll have no choice but to succumb." Up until that moment, I'd been in two minds about doing a bunk. Now I knew I had no choice. But where would I go? "Edward? Edward!" I grabbed my bag and searched for my mobile. It was gone. Mum had taken it. I waited until they'd gone to bed and crept out onto the landing. I removed the land-line handset from its docking-bay and returned to my room.

I called Edward's mobile and prayed that it was switched on. It went straight to voice mail. After the beep, I whispered, "For God's sake, Edward! Look, I need to talk to you. It's urgent. You can't call on my mobile because the olds have it. And you can't ring this number because you'll wake them. Listen, I'll try you again in about ten minutes. *Please* pick up when I do."

Chapter 30

I tried Edward's mobile every five minutes for the next hour. At 1am, he finally answered it. I said, "Thank God! What the hell have you been doing?"

"Sorry, Babe. I'm here now." I told him that I was under house-arrest until the morning when I was to be frog-marched to a clinic. Following a stunned pause, Edward said, "… How did it go with Ken?"

I told him it had gone great and that I needed to abscond to a place where I could continue the fight beyond the gaze of others.

Edward said, "Scotland!" The urgency in his voice suggested he'd just heard of Scotland's destruction. Then he reminded me that his parents owned a time-share apartment in a converted castle in Loch Lomond. He said, "We haven't been able to use it this year and I think … I mean, I'm not certain of the dates but it might be empty ..."

"Can you check?"

"I'm headed for the kitchen. There's a calendar on the wall that … wait … we still have nine days of access left, Hally."

"What about the keys?"

Edward went and opened a cupboard in the hall. I heard keys being handled and discarded. Finally, he said, "I have the keys. Are you sure about this?"

"I don't feel I have a choice. Anna's re-grouping, she's getting stronger ... I need space to fight her."

Edward has a motorbike. I've never liked riding on it. Even short journeys tended to freak me out. Edward said, "Are you going to be okay on the bike? Scotland's a long haul."

"I'll have to be. Get yourself over here. I'll climb down the drain pipe." I hung up the phone and wrote mum and dad the following note:

'Sorry! I love you both very much and know that you mean well and are doing your best to understand what I'm going through.

Please believe me, this is something I have to do. It's MY life in the balance and I want to be rid of Anna more than anything. I'll be back in a week or so and I'll do whatever you want me to. But I have to try it my way first.' I wrote down Edward's mobile number and signed the note.

Chapter 31

I dragged the suitcase that mum had so thoughtfully packed for my trip, over to the window. Not long after, a silhouette of a man pushing a motorbike came into view. At first, I thought that something must be wrong with the infernal machine. Then I remembered what a racket it made and decided to award the boy full marks for ingenuity.

Edward stood the bike on its stand and walked over to the drainpipe. I stuck my head out of the window and whispered, "Mum's packed a suitcase for the trip. Think you can catch it? It's not so heavy."

Edward looked up and whispered, "Sure!" He held out his hands. I heaved the suitcase up onto the window sill. The next moment, there was a horrid *thud*. I peered down to see Edward crouched on the ground, rubbing his back. I asked him if he was okay and he said that he would be.

My helmet was at least three sizes too big. We set off and my head rattled around inside it like beach-ball in a tumble dryer. Edward was thoughtful enough to pull over every hour to let me re-align my brain, stretch my legs and check that the suitcase was still securely fastened to the rack behind me. Several noisy hours later, we arrived at our destination: Loch Lomond, Scotland.

The converted castle was beautiful. We roared up its gravel driveway and came to a shuddering stop outside an open portcullis. It was 7am and the only people about were gardeners tending to a rose-garden. The scent of the roses was sweet and comforting and added to my desire to sleep. We hauled our luggage up a spiral staircase and onto a landing. The apartment was small, decorated in paisleys and overlooked a lake to the rear of the castle. We collapsed onto the double bed. Edward put his arm around me. I guess I felt okay about that, so I turned toward him and placed my head on his chest. "I'm so sorry."

He hugged me close. "What have you done now?"

"I mean it. I'm sorry for not trusting you. My *head* ..."

"It's okay. Like you said, your head ..."

"It's like ... like I've been locked in a room with only Anna for company for *months*. And everything else .... I mean all the *positive stuff* ... you, my family, my friends, ambitions ... Anna put outside the room. It was like you all became distant, vague ... *outside*."

"I get it. Okay?" He kissed the top of my head.

"You couldn't get it ... not unless you knew what it felt like to be locked in a room with only a crazy bitch for company."

I suppose he could have made a pretty funny joke about that. I was glad he didn't. Instead he said, "Maybe you should write it down ... let people know what this feels like."

"I'm not that clever."

"Ah, yes, you are." I fanned my fingers out over his heart. And we fell asleep.

Chapter 32

A couple of hours later, Edward's mobile rang. I opened my eyes, saw him reaching for it. I said, "It's probably mum. I left her your number."

Edward read the caller's number on the display. He handed me his phone. I answered it. "Hello?"

Mum said, "Come home right now, Hally!"

"You must have read my note?"

"Stop trying my patience, Hally."

"I need to take the fight to Anna, Mum. All I'm asking for is one week. I just need you to trust me for seven days! Surely you can do that?"

Mum said, "I'm trying, Hally. I really am."

"Could you try a little bit harder, please. It is MY life on the line here."

"Where are you?"

"I'm with Edward and we're fine. I'm sorry, Mum. I'll call you in a couple of days." I hung up and switched off the phone.

Sometime later, I woke to sunshine streaming through the half-drawn curtains. Edward nibbled my shoulder. He said, "I'm starving."

I said, "You can't eat that ... I'm going to need it later." I sat up. "Believe it or not, I'm hungry too."

I climbed off the bed and drew back the curtains. The sun reflected off the lake outside. I squinted and said, "How big are the woods around the lake?"

Edward said, "Enormous. I got lost in them once. "

I said, "We need to pack a lunch. Then we need to find a secluded spot where I can draw Anna out ..." I swallowed hard, "to fight me." Edward told me it was turning into the weirdest experience of his life, and that he couldn't imagine sharing it with anyone else. I decided not to thank him and headed for the shower.

When I came out of the bathroom, Edward was standing by the front door of the apartment holding his motorcycle helmet. He said, "Any preference for lunch?"

I said, "No. Just make sure whatever you bring back is dripping in fat, sugar, or both."

He nodded and left.

I retrieved the hand-grip from my bag and placed it on a small table beside an armchair. I sat down in the chair and stared at it. Anna loomed from the shadows in such a way that she made me shudder. She said, *"You got lucky last time. You do know that, don't you?"* She sounded strong again. Not as strong as she once was, but strong enough to cause me to reach for the hand-grip. She said, *"You don't need that. All I want you to do is think about the fatty, sugary foods you've asked Edward to bring back. You need to consider what's going to happen to you if you eat them."*

I thought, 'I'll feel less hollow. Less of a freak?'

"You'll become even more of a freak. A fat freak. Edward will start seeing Charlotte."

I caught myself nodding in agreement. I stood up, moved swiftly to the window, and looked for any sign of Edward. Anna said, *"You don't actually think the boy's coming back, do you? You've frightened him off for good with your insane babblings. If he wasn't convinced you were a total nut job before he sure is now. Which means you're alone, with only me to protect you. Just like it should be. Just like it will always be."*

My hands were trembling. "Of *course* Edward's coming back."

"You need to go into the bathroom and look in the mirror."

Through gritted teeth I said, "Just. Leave. Me. Alone."

Anna said, *"You know I can't let you do this. You've already become such a disappointment to your family. Your being here with Edward is destroying them. They're the ones who care about you. Not Edward. Mum and dad have sacrificed so much for you. And what do you do? Even after everything you've put them through, you go and pull this. You're a disgusting person. Not only do you want to get fat, you are selfish. Maybe you should do the world a favour? The fall from that window would do it. Snap your fat neck. You'll start to lose weight like never before. Death. It's the ultimate diet.*

We should try it. Might as well. You want out? Well, death is the only way out of Anna's hunger games."

I muttered, "Come on, Edward. Come *on*. Please."

Anna said, *"There are some scales in the bathroom."*

I caught myself turning towards the bathroom. I froze. Tears stung my eyes. I thought, 'No ... *when* Edward gets back, we're going into the woods ... and I'm going to *kill you*.'

Anna said, *"We both know that's not going to happen. You got lucky last time. Caught me by surprise. And even then you* just *managed to resist me. That's because I wasn't expecting a fight. I had my guard down. But it's different now, Hally. I have a new set of tactics. I'm so ready for you. You imagine you know what hell feels like? Well, think again. Because if you go through with this insane plan to defy me, well, let's just say, you'll wish you* were *dead."* I stumbled to the phone on the bedside table and called Ken.

Ken's comforting voice said, "Hello ..."

I babbled, "It's me, Ken. It's Hally. I'm in Scotland. My boyfriend has gone off to get food. When he comes back, I'm going to take the fight to Anna ...like you taught me but ..."

"But she's telling you that she'll be ready for you this time? That it was just a fluke that you got the better of her the last time? That you're doomed to failure?"

"Yes, yes .... what should I do?"

"Calm down and listen to me, Hally. Her threats are hollow. They hold no weight whatsoever. She's just trying to make you balk. She wants you to give up before you've even begun. Just stand firm, Hally. Stick to your guns. And when she charges you will beat her."

I babbled, "But how do you know that?"

"I know she *relies* upon your collapsing under her onslaught of doubts and horrid feelings. She *needs* you to give up, *balk*, and simply abandon your counter attack. Listen ... there comes a point in *her* attack when she has used so much energy in yanking those levers, that she has no choice BUT to back down. You, on the other hand, have hidden reserves of energy and determination that can carry you well past that point ... to *victory*."

I felt emotional. I said, "I mustn't cry ... it's important that I don't cry, isn't it, Ken?"

"Get angry, Hally. Leave the luxury of tears until after your next triumph."

I heard Edward's motorbike growling up the driveway outside.

I said, "Thank God for you, Ken."

Ken told me that he had utmost faith in me. We hung up.

Chapter 33

We set off into the woods.

Edward carried a food hamper he'd bought in the village: a wicker basket filled with Anna bait. It was a humid day. Midges and bumble bees floated and buzzed beneath the forest's canopy. Edward pointed out a place he thought would be ideal for kicking Anna's butt. I agreed, it was perfect. A secluded little clearing surrounded by tall trees. Edward put down the hamper, collapsed onto his bottom and leaned forwards, grasping his ankles.

I said, "Sorry about dropping my suitcase on you yesterday. Is your back okay?"

He smiled and beckoned me to come and sit next to him. Edward said, "So, here we are. The scene of your greatest triumph."

"Or my most embarrassing disaster."

"What's to be embarrassed about? You've come here, to beautiful Scotland, to do battle with a voice in your head called Anna. No biggie. You think you're the first?"

"Ah, *yeah*."

He hugged me close and said, "I've got your back. You do know that?"

I nodded and tapped out a little rhythm on the hamper's lid. Several butterflies spawned in my belly and fluttered to my impromptu drum session. I said, "What's in here, exactly? What's the bait?"

Edward opened the lid to reveal a Tartan enclosure stuffed with food, plates and cutlery. My butterflies spawned some children. I knew I should reach for the hand-grip and expel them from my tummy but, for some reason, I balked. Edward attempted to sound light hearted. "So? What do you fancy? A chicken drumstick? A sausage roll? Pork pie? Perhaps you'd like to skip the main course and go straight to dessert? We have strawberry cheesecake, which is your favourite."

I gazed down inside the hamper, and grimaced. "You certainly know your stuff when it comes to Anna bait."

"I do my best. You all right?"

"... Well, apart from a few butterflies ... I feel … okay."

"You did say you'd given Anna a good beating. Perhaps it was a more complete ass kicking than you imagined? Maybe you've conquered her already?"

"Now wouldn't that be nice. No. I had a chat with her this morning. She paid me a visit after you left … wanted me to go and fixate on my body in the bathroom, weigh myself … and worse."

"And did you? Weigh yourself?"

"No. I did not."

Edward asked if she had tried to *force* me to weigh myself. I told him she hadn't. "I suspect she was saving her energy, you know, for the next time I tried to eat something against her will."

We both gazed down inside the hamper, and shuffled nervously. It was Edward's turn to swallow hard now. He said, "What do you want me to do? You know, if you start to freak-out."

"Well, if you could just try not to laugh ..."

He hugged me again and kissed my forehead.

I stood up clutching a drumstick in one hand and my hand-grip in the other. Edward took a couple of steps back, as though he'd just lit a dangerous firework. I lifted the chicken drumstick to eye level, gazed at it. I felt completely fine and, following a fateful shrug of my shoulders, I tore a strip of succulent meat off with my teeth. I was literally starving and it tasted delicious. I moaned and gasped with pleasure. Edward placed his mobile against his ear. Again, I sighed in delight and subjected the drumstick to another mauling. Then I asked Edward who he was calling. He said, "The ambulance service. Nobody should have to suffer in this way without some medical back-up."

I said, "I don't know what the deal is! Maybe she just wants to make me look stupid." Edward suggested that she was doing an excellent job so far. I finished the drumstick and immediately ate another. Then I tucked into a pork pie. Edward opened a can of cola and I swigged that down, too. Then I ate a packet of crisps and a slice of cheesecake. I sat down on a tree-root and belched. I *really did* feel bloated and it was an entirely different feeling to the one Anna often created with her expert mix of chemicals. This feeling was warm and comforting and it occurred to me that compulsive over-eaters must have an Anna of their own, only in reverse – a voice that pushed them *towards* food, towards this comforting feeling, rather than away from it.

I burped again and Edward said he was going for a pee. I gazed up into the thick canopy of trees. Anna seemed to swoop down out of them, "*... You're all alone now ... like a helpless little lamb ... listen ... isn't that a wolf I can hear ... ?*"

I thought, 'No. I'm not alone. And the only *wolf* around here is the psychotic dog in my head.'

Anna said, "*After everything I've done for you. You ungrateful little ...*" Anna reached for her levers. I felt a pang of nausea, and scrambled to my feet holding the hand-grip. Anna and I were like a couple of gunfighters, willing the other to draw first. Anna had the advantage – until she unleashed her first wave of proper hell, I would have no target to blast with feel-good endorphins. But I sensed her close now, circling me, trying to decide which direction to charge from: panic, anxiety or ballooning?

Edward came back, pulling up his zipper. He was about to speak but I hushed him. He sat down on the tree-root and stared at me. I muttered, "Come on, Anna. Let's see what you've got." I was growing impatient and I heard myself cry out, "Come on, Anna! I said show me what you got!" Some birds took flight from the trees about us. Edward looked as though he would have liked to have joined them.

Anna said, "*Edward thinks you've lost the plot. Who could blame him? And do you have any idea how many calories you've just consumed? Thousands. They're clogging up your arteries with fat and blubber and ... you fell right into my trap! You disgust me. You* are *disgusting. And you're going to vomit it all back up or you'll burst!*" Anna charged from the darkest corners of my mind, and buried her horns of anxiety and panic *deep* into me.

I doubled over, *literally* ... and gulped for the air I needed as ammo. Ammo? Yeah, I needed ammo. Air in my lungs with which to exhale the army of butterflies Anna had just puked up in there. Horror of horrors, I found myself retching! Anna, that cunning spiteful bitch, had *wrestled* control of my breathing away from me. I thought, 'I'm screwed! She's going to force me to hurl!'

I coughed and spluttered and heard Edward yell, "Don't do it, Hally! Don't throw up! Fight her!"

I gave him a stinging look that said, 'the thought had occurred to me,' and fell to one knee, huffing and puffing, trying to get control over my breathing with short, sharp exhales – like a woman in the throes of labour.

Meanwhile, Anna's bellowing, *"Give in! Empty your belly! You know you want to! You'll feel such relief! You'll be less of a disappointment to everyone! Less of a failure. Less gross!"* Puff by puff, I clawed back control of my breathing; and started crushing the butterflies with my abs … slowly but surely, I was making the feel-good endorphins I needed to fight her – a feeling of relief replaced the gnawing sickness in my gut. Man, that was all the encouragement I needed. I stood up and let rip – transformed myself into Hally, the growling, frowning, stomping bitch of the wood. No longer a cowering victim, but a female warrior fighting for her life.

At some point, I actually threw down the hand-grip and picked up a large stick. I have a vague recollection of Edward asking me what I was doing as I sprinted towards a bank of stinging nettles and slashed and tore into them screaming, "Come on, Anna! You crazy bitch! Come and get me! What are you waiting for!? Charge me!" Pretty soon, my stomach muscles were in *agony*. Just like I'd been having the longest, most hysterical belly laugh imaginable. But I didn't care about that. Compared to the pain of anxiety and fear it was actually welcome. I imagined those nettles *were* Anna as I tore into them, my positive adrenaline driving me on, and masking the pain of the countless nettle stings on my wrists and knuckles. Anna put up a good fight. But I put up a *better* one.

Ken had been right. If I refused to balk, *refused* to back down, stuck to my guns, and kept producing positive adrenaline, then Anna would have no choice but to back off and re-group to fight another day. Just like she'd done in the classroom below the church.

Following a couple of minutes of serious violence, the bank of nettles was ripped to shreds and Anna skulked off into the shadows, to lick her wounds.

That day she charged me three more times. With each charge, I felt her weakening, but my resolve remained the same. I was merciless. I wanted her blood. Simple as. The next day we returned to the same spot in the woods with our picnic, but Anna didn't even show up. On days three and four she entered my arena and fought me again. But I had the measure of her now. Each attack was more desperate, more feeble than the last.

The turning point came on day five when it felt as though I was being attacked by a weakened child. When she charged, all I needed to do was grab the top of her head and hold her at arm's length. I almost felt sorry for her as she swung weak punches at me, punches that amounted to a single, baby butterfly in my tummy. Eventually, she stopped swinging and collapsed to her knees. Her voice was so feeble that it was barely audible. She said, "*Hally, please listen ... I need you to trust me again. I've only ever wanted to help you. I've only ever wanted to protect you. I beg you ... please ... do as I say. Stop fighting me. Avoid food. Starve yourself. It is the only way. Please, Hally ... you're killing me. I'm fading. I don't want to die ... I don't want to leave you alone. What will you do without me?*"

I murmured, "Live."

That night, I fell asleep in Edward's arms. I dreamed about going to see Ken at St. Luke's church. In the graveyard, I spotted a row of new graves. I realised these graves contained my past fears. The first headstone read: **R.I.P. Fear of the bogey man in the closet.**

I walked along to another, it read:

R.I.P. Fear of Sarah becoming mum and dad's favourite daughter now.

And another that read:

R.I.P. Fear of not being accepted at school.

I passed several more, and then stopped by a freshly dug grave. It was empty. Piles of earth lay round its edges, ready to be shovelled in. This headstone loomed higher than the others and read: **R.I.P. Anna Rexia.**

Ken was suddenly standing beside me. He said, "You've won the toughest battles against Anna. If you continue to fight the good fight, it won't be long before you've won the war, Hally." He stabbed a finger at the empty grave. "And Anna will be where she can no longer harm you. Ever."

I said, "I really fought her, Ken. I thought I might bust a gut or something."

Ken squeezed my shoulder, "We'd all need to bust a gut to defeat the likes of Anna." Then he pointed to a row of vacant plots beside Anna's.

"Who are they for?" I asked.

Ken magicked a couple of chocolate biscuits from thin air. As we nibbled he said, "Those are for your future fears. Whatever they are, whatever is coming … if you refuse to run, refuse to back down, they can't bully and control you. Just like Anna couldn't."

That advice Ken gave me in my dream? Well, it goes for you too. Whoever you are, wherever you're reading this, please don't let your fears ruin your life. Stand up to any voice in your head, or any *feelings* in your body, that won't let you be happy. Won't let you *forget*. Take the fight to them, and *prise* their fingers off those trap-door levers. If you fight and refuse to back down? … Well, I know for sure, you'll win the battles ahead.

THE END

Anna's Hunger Games was inspired by a true story.
This book is dedicated to the memory of Ken Payne.
1924-2006

Printed in Great Britain
by Amazon